Peter Dickinson's

The Kin

MANA'S STORY

Peter Dickinson's

The Kin

MANA'S STORY

PUTNAM & GROSSET • NEW YORK

Library of Congress Cataloging-in-Publication Data
Dickinson, Peter, 1927-
Mana's story.
p.   cm — (Peter Dickinson's The kin)
Companion volume to: Noli's story, Suth's story, and Po's story.
Summary: Mana and the other Kin, a band of people living in prehistoric
times, search for food on the edge of a great marsh and fight a new enemy,
the dangerous killers whom they name the demon men.
[1. Prehistoric peoples—Fiction. 2. Survival—Fiction.] I. Title. II. Series:
Dickinson, Peter, 1927-   Kin.
PZ7.D562Man   1998   [Fic]—dc21   98-47030   CIP   AC

ISBN 0-399-23350-4
A B C D E F G H I J

For Rosemary and George

Peter Dickinson's

The Kin

MANA'S STORY

Before you start....

About two hundred thousand years ago, on a hot continent, the first true, modern human beings evolved. There were other humans before them, and living alongside them, but these were our direct ancestors. Some experts believe the one thing that made them different from these other humans was that they had language. They spoke in words.

They have left very few traces—fossils of their bones and the bones of the animals they ate, rough stone tools, the ashes of their fires, not much else. What were they like? How did they live and speak and think? Even the experts can only guess, so that's what I've done, too. One of my guesses is that they told stories to explain why things are the way they are and remember what happened long ago. I've put some of these "Oldtales" between chapters, as a way of telling how these early people may have thought about their world.

This book is about a girl called Mana. She belongs to the Moonhawk Kin. They and the seven other Kins used to live in what they now call the Old Good Places, but five years ago they were driven from there by a horde of murderous strangers. Only half the Moonhawks, with a few people from the other Kins, survived. After various adventures, which you can read about in *Suth's Story* and *Noli's Story*, they reached the New Good Places, and settled down there.

Po's Story told how a terrible drought forced them to move again, and find their way across an immense marsh with the help of the strange marshpeople. Now they have reached the northern edge of the marsh, and are preparing to travel on once more.

—Peter Dickinson

1

Mana was fishing, alone, among the reeds.

She had her own fishing hole. Suth and Tor had helped her make a path into the reedbed, laying the cut reeds flat on the net of roots for her to walk on. Ten and ten paces in they had made a small clearing, and in the middle of this they had cut a circular hole down through the roots, leaving a little pool of clear water, less than a pace across.

They'd known what to do because Po had seen one of the marshwomen fishing like this. But after that they'd had to find things out for themselves—what sort of bait was best; how a target in the water was never where the eye saw it, but higher; and, most important of all, how to wait and wait in utter stillness, and then fling the power of every muscle in arm and shoulder and side into a strike as quick and sudden as the strike of a snake. Any twitch, any hesitation before that moment, and the fish would startle, and flick away. Mana was good at waiting.

Tinu had found the trick of it first, and shown the others. Then Suth had made the children practice and practice. He'd put a leaf on the end of a thin reed and moved it around under the water, as a fish might move, and they'd used that for a target. When Mana's fishing stick pierced the leaf three times out of four, time and time again, Suth and Tor made the path for her.

So now for the first time she crouched by her own

fishing hole, with her stick—a strong reedstem, sharpened to a point—resting on her shoulder, ready for the
strike. This part of the reedbeds was full of fish. It was
strange that none of the marshpeople came here to
catch them, but they seemed wary of being so close to
the shore, as if there was something here that scared
them badly.

Mana could see three little fish, silver with a green
stripe along the side, the size of her middle finger. That
was good. They were much too small to spear, but their
movements would tell larger fish that there was food
here. Gently she edged her left hand forward and dribbled another few dragonfly eggs onto the surface. As
the white specks wavered down through the water, the
little fish darted at them and sucked them in. Two more
fish appeared from the darkness beneath the reeds, one
the same sort and the other slightly larger, dark brown
and blunt nosed.

Was that a movement, a shadowy something stirring
at the edge of the darkness?

Mana's heart started to pump. More slowly than ever
she drifted her left hand forward and dropped a few
more of the precious eggs. The shadow came nosing out
to take them, a fish as long as a man's foot, deep-bellied,
blue-black with a red spot behind the eye. It was too
late. The little fish had gotten there first.

Mana released another dribble of eggs. All six fish
rose for them, competing, and began to follow them
down.

Now!

As the dark back turned away, Mana struck. The
point jarred for an instant against a toughness, but she
drove it on. At once the spear came alive in her grip,
snatching itself back and forth as the fish fought to
wrench itself free. Hands and arms remembered their

endless lessons, so she didn't make the instinctive move, pulling the stick back at the same angle at which she'd thrust it in—that would risk pulling it out of the fish—but grabbed it with her left hand as far forward as she could reach, and then pulled up and sideways, leaning her body back to heave the stick out with its point just clearing the far edge of the hole. A handsbreadth down it, pierced clean through, the fish flailed in the air.

With a sigh of happiness Mana rose and stood, absentmindedly brushing insects from her body. They'd swarmed around and on her all the time she was fishing, but she'd scarcely noticed them. Several had bitten her. She could imagine how she'd be itching by nightfall, but she didn't mind. It was all so worth it. At her first try, at her own new fishing hole, she'd caught this beautiful fish.

She forced the stick farther through it so that it couldn't wriggle itself free, then laid it on the path. When the water was still, she took a different sort of bait from her gourd—not the dragonfly eggs, which were hard to find, but crumbs of the stuff left over after pounding blueroot paste—and sprinkled them onto the hole. They floated on the surface, so that the fish that had been frightened away would find them when they came back and think this was a good place to look for food again. The one fish she'd caught was enough for Mana, enough happiness, enough food for herself and someone else. She put her stick over her shoulder with the fish hanging behind her, and left.

Now, climbing the hill, she realized how glad she was to escape from the marsh insects. This happened every time anyone went into the marsh. Clouds of the horrible creatures gathered around them in the steamy heat, mostly just to settle and tickle as they drank their sweat, but some to bite in and suck their blood. They had all learned to put up with it, to forget about it as they did what they were there for. But as soon as they could, they climbed back up the hill into the fresher, drier heat, where the insects mostly didn't come.

When Mana was high enough she sat down to wait. Now, of course, more than anything, she wanted to show someone her lovely fish, but they were all busy fishing at various fish holes in the huge reedbed that reached along the shoreline below her. She'd chosen a place where she could see anyone who came out, so that she could run at once and show them. But she wasn't impatient for them to come. She was happy to wait, happy in her own happiness, not needing anyone to share it.

The hill on which she was sitting was like the tail of some vast crocodile, a craggy, steep-sided promontory rising to a central ridge, where the crocodile's spine would have been. From north to south the promontory was a whole difficult day's journey in length.

Mana was sitting on its eastern side, with the morning sun shining in her face. In front of her and to her right, the mist-veiled marshes stretched away. Somewhere out there Var and Net and Yova and Kern should now be making their way back from the far side, using the paths that the marshmen had shown them.

They had gone to get fresh supplies of salt. They'd used up almost all of what they'd brought with them as gifts for the marshmen, and Tun had decided they might need more, to help make friends with any new people they met when they journeyed north to look for new places where they could live. It was something to do while they waited for everyone to recover from the marsh sickness.

Two of them had died—Runa, and Moru's little

daughter Taja. Most of the others had been very sick. Mana had been the first, before they'd even started to cross. Chogi said that it was from sleeping in the marshes, or too near them. But now everybody was well again, though some were still a bit weak, and as soon as the salt expedition returned they would be ready to travel north.

Mana felt anxious about the move. She knew they couldn't stay here for ever. Plant food was already getting scarce along the shorelines, and they couldn't live on fish alone. Besides, this wasn't the sort of life they were used to. But Mana didn't really like change. She preferred things she knew and understood. That was one of the reasons she'd been so pleased about catching her fish—it meant that there was something useful she could do. Fishing gave her a place among the Kin, a purpose. And now that she thought about it, she felt suddenly sad that soon she would be leaving her fishing hole. She would be going to places where, perhaps, she would never have the chance to fish again.

She rose and looked north, along the way they were going to travel. Tun had sent scouts up there to explore. They'd come back and reported that after half a day's journey they had not reached the end of the promontory. It had become steadily steeper until one side was almost a cliff, with neither space nor soil for anything much to grow between the plunging rock face and the marsh.

So now Mana gazed along the hillside, trying to imagine the difficult journey, and wondering what might lie at the end of it. Would it be a great wide-open landscape, perhaps with a river running through it, and clumps of shade trees and patches of bushes, like the Good Places she could just remember, before the rains had failed?

The imaginary landscape filled her mind, so she wasn't really studying the actual one that lay in front of her. Even so, a quick movement caught her eye. She stiffened, and stared.

Yes, there. Brief, furtive, a brown flicker between two boulders. Gone.

A fox or a jackal? Too big. Not a deer's motion. Anyway, they'd seen no creatures that size in this place. The promontory was too barren for grazing animals, and there wasn't enough prey for the meat eaters.

There again! Though Mana saw it clearly this time she still couldn't tell what it was. A round black head, a brown back behind it, the movements rapid but awkward...

Only when it had vanished did she realize what she'd seen. The creature slinking up the hillside was human—a woman, Mana thought—one of the marsh-people, judging by the color of her skin. She was moving in that strange way because she was crouching low and at the same time clutching something in both her hands, held close to her chest....

There she was again. But her hands weren't clutching something. They were holding it cupped between the palms. The woman paused, peering around a boulder, not toward Mana but away from her, north, as though she was hiding from a danger that might be coming from that direction. She scuttled on, still with the same awkward gait as she tried not to spill whatever she was carrying.

It could only be water, Mana decided. Why was a marshwoman carrying water up over the barren rocks? The marshpeople never came out onto the promontory. There was something out here they were desperately afraid of—and certainly the way the woman was behaving showed that she shared that fear. And why was she carrying water in her hands, instead of in one of the reed tubes that the marshpeople used for that sort of thing?

Curious, Mana picked up her fishing stick, with the fish still impaled on it, and set off across the hillside. She wasn't afraid. The marshwomen were pleasant and easy to deal with, and the men weren't dangerous, for all their proud ways. But since the woman had been moving so warily, Mana slipped behind a boulder the moment she reappeared, and waited until she was well down the hillside before moving on.

When she was near the place from which the woman had come, she laid her stick down and crawled silently on until she could peep around a rock to see what lay beyond.

She looked down into a small, steep-sided hollow. At the bottom lay a man. His eyes were shut. His face was pulled into tight lines of pain. Blood oozed from a ghastly wound below his left shoulder. His right arm was flung out across the stony ground. A small boy, almost a baby, sat clutching his fingers and staring around with a look of terror, misery, and bewilderment.

The man's face wasn't painted with bright colors, as the marshmen's always were. Nor did he wear their kind of braided reed-leaf belt with wooden tubes dangling from it. These weren't marshpeople after all.

It didn't cross Mana's mind that these people had nothing to do with her, and she didn't have to help them. The look on both their faces told her she must. She glanced down the hill and saw the woman already starting to climb back up with a few more precious mouthfuls of water for the wounded man. Better wait for her.

Mana crept a little way back and hid, but as soon as the woman had vanished into the hollow she eased the fish off her stick and crawled with it to where she could look down again.

The woman was crouched over the man, dribbling water onto his mouth. Half of it splashed aside, but his tongue came out and lapped the rest in. When the water was almost gone she held the last palmful in front of the boy and pushed his face down into it so that he could suck it up. Mana waited until she'd finished, then hissed softly.

Instantly the woman spun around, snatched up rocks with both hands, and crouched snarling in front of the man.

Mana kneeled with her hand held palm forward in the sign of peace and greeting. The woman stayed where she was, with her teeth bared, snarling like a cornered jackal. Mana held out the fish and made the double hum that people who didn't have words used to mean *I give*.

The woman frowned, uncertain, and stopped snarling, but stayed in her fighting crouch with her eyes flickering from side to side. Mana smiled, shrugged, and flipped the fish down into the hollow. It landed at the woman's feet.

The woman hesitated, staring back and forth between Mana and the fish. Finally she made up her mind, dropped the rock from her left hand, and without taking her eyes off Mana, groped for the fish. Still in her fighting pose, with the rock in her right hand ready to fling, she bit a mouthful out of the back, chewed it, spat the chewings into her hand, and forced them between the man's lips. He munched feebly while she chewed some for the child.

Not taking her eyes from Mana she took a mouthful for herself, and while she chewed it, backed up to the far side of the hollow until she could see out over the rim. Here at last she turned and scanned the hillside to the north, but kept glancing around at Mana to make sure she hadn't moved. Then she came back and went on feeding the three of them.

This would obviously take some time, so Mana emptied the contents of her gourd onto a flat rock and hurried down the hillside, keeping under cover just as she'd seen the woman doing. Judging by the man's wound, they had every reason to be afraid. She filled the gourd at a marsh pool and carried it back up.

This time she picked her way down into the hollow. The woman snarled and got ready to strike, but Mana smiled at her and showed her the gourd, brimming with water. The woman hesitated, so Mana put the gourd down and climbed back out of the hollow. The woman relaxed a little, picked up the gourd, and started to help the man drink from it.

Mana turned and looked south along the shore. Two people had now come out of the reedbed. Even at that distance she recognized the smaller one as Po. No one else had that special sort of look-at-me way of standing, eager and uncertain at the same time. The other one looked like Moru. Po was showing her something. He looked proud and happy about it. He must have had luck with his fishing too.

With a pang Mana realized that now she could never show anybody her beautiful first fish. By the time these strangers finished with it there would be nothing left but the bones. But she'd had to give it to them. There'd been nothing else she could have done. And now she had to go and bring help for them. That was obvious too.

She called softly to the woman, pointed, smiled and made the *I go* sound. The woman didn't react. Mana wondered whether she used the same noises as the other wordless people she knew. She had made no sounds at all so far, except for snarls.

In fact, Mana realized as she hurried across the slope, she didn't know anything about these people at all. If they hadn't been in such trouble when she'd found them, would they have been friends or enemies? She couldn't tell.

All she knew was they were in desperate need, and in danger. She could even guess, from the man's wound, what sort of danger that might be. It wasn't the bite or the claw mark of some big fierce animal. Something hard and sharp had struck the man a savage blow, and driven deep into him. It might have been the horn of an animal, but the wound looked too wide to have been made by any antelope Mana had ever seen. And if it had been something like that, why should the woman be so deadly afraid, so instantly ready to fight? An antelope didn't chase down the hunter it had wounded.

No, Mana thought. People had made that wound. She had never seen a wound from the thrust of a digging stick, but that was what it would look like.

This is bad, she thought, *bad*. Now perhaps she and all her friends were in the same danger as the three she had left in the hollow. But she still felt she couldn't have done anything else.

Oldtale

The Dilli Hunt

Black Antelope slept. His sleep was long, long.

Fat Pig and Snake drank stoneweed. They were happy.

Snake boasted. He said, "See my man Gul. No hunter is swifter. No hunter has keener eyes. He throws a rock. No hunter has truer aim."

Fat Pig said, "Snake, you lie. My man Dop is better. He strikes a rock with his digging stick. It shatters apart. He follows the track of the dilli buck. He does not lose it. In the dark night he smells it."

Snake said, "Fat Pig, you lie. Gul is better."

They quarrelled. Their voices were loud.

Weaver said, "You two, stop your shouting. My wives cannot hear my orders."

Fat Pig and Snake said, "Judge between us, Weaver. See our men Gul and Dop. Which is the better hunter?"

Weaver looked from the top of the Mountain, the Mountain above Odutu.

He said, "See that fine dilli buck. He has a black patch on his rump. Go now. Make him two. Now you have two dilli bucks. Set one before Dop. Set one before Gul. Make each dilli buck run to Yellowspring. One man comes there first. He kills his buck. That man is the better hunter."

Fat Pig and Snake said, "Weaver, this is good. We do it."

But Weaver said in his heart, *This is nothing to me, which hunter is better. Yellowspring is far and far. Now we have quiet here.*

Gul hunted. Dop hunted. Each saw a fine dilli buck. It had a black patch on its rump. It ran before them. It was clever. It turned aside, it ran on rock, it hid in thick bushes. The hunters did not lose the tracks. The bucks came near Yellowspring. Both came there together, but Dop followed closer.

Snake saw this. He was not happy. He said in his heart, *My man loses the contest. We made two bucks from one. Now I make one from two.*

He put a stoneweed in Fat Pig's path. Fat Pig found it. He drank. He did not watch the hunt. Snake caused Dop's buck to run behind a thicket. Then he made two bucks into one. Dop's buck was gone.

Dop came behind the thicket. His buck was not there. Its tracks ended. He hunted this way and that. He could not find it.

Gul followed his buck to Yellowspring. There he killed it. He was happy.

Dop was thirsty. He went to Yellowspring. He saw Gul. He saw the dead buck. It had a black patch on its rump.

Dop said, "Gul, you killed my buck. All day I hunted it."

Gul said, "Dop, you lie. The buck is mine. All day I hunted it."

Dop took the buck by the hind legs. Gul took the buck by the forelegs. Both pulled. Neither was stronger.

Gul took one hand from the buck. He picked up a rock. He flung it. His aim was good. The rock struck Dop on the side of his jaw. He loosened his hold on the buck.

It was sudden. Gul was not ready. He went backward. His foot caught on a grass clump. He fell.

Dop leaped at Gul. He struck at him with his digging stick, a fierce blow. Gul twisted aside. Dop's digging stick drove into the ground.

Gul laughed. He said, "Dop, an anteater is swifter, a blind anteater."

He struck at Dop, a fierce blow. Dop turned it aside. He laughed. He said, "Gul, a nestling is stronger, a featherless nestling."

Each mocked the other. They were filled with rage, the rage of heroes. They fought.

Snake and Fat Pig saw this. They said, "This is good. Now we see which is better."

All day Dop and Gul fought. They gave fierce blows. They threw rocks. They struck with their fists. They bit with their mouths. Blood flowed.

The sun sank low. Gul saw this. He turned away. He ran toward the sun. Dop followed.

Now Gul turned again. He faced Dop. He struck him a great blow, the blow of a hero. It was like this:

See this tree, this father of trees. No tree is taller, none stronger. Now is the time of rains. See this cloud. It is black, it is slow, it is filled with thunder. It stands over the father of trees. It bursts. Out of it falls the lightning. The sun is not brighter. The lion's roar is not louder. The father of trees is stricken, he falls, he lies on the ground.

Such was Gul's blow at Dop.

The sun was in Dop's eyes. He did not see Gul's blow. It struck him on the head, the side of the head, behind the eye. His sight was darkened. His knees were weak. He fell to the ground. He did not move

Gul picked up the dilli buck. He carried it away. He was happy.

2

The man couldn't stand, let alone walk, so Suth and Net linked hands to make a seat, and with his arms around their shoulders they carried him moaning back to the camp. His wound reopened and bled the whole way. The woman seemed to have decided that these strangers were friendly. She walked anxiously beside the man, carrying the child and glancing back over her shoulder every few steps.

They made the man as comfortable as they could on a bed of reedstems, and Mana fetched water for the woman to wash his wound, and then put what was left of her fish on the ashes of the fire to roast for them.

It was time for the midday rest, but first Tun sent Po and Nar to keep a watch to the north, one on either side of the hill. The others sat in the shade, eating what they had caught or found, and talking in low voices about the strangers. Mana couldn't hear what the men were saying on the far side of the fire, but the women around her all agreed that the man's wound had been made by something like a digging stick and that the woman was very scared. They guessed it was because whoever had caused the wound might be following them.

Nobody said a word of blame to Mana for what she had done. Like her, they all seemed to feel that she'd had no choice.

Before the rest ended, Mana went up the hill with Shuja to take over as lookouts. They stayed there most of the afternoon, until Zara came up with Dipu to relieve them. As they were making their way back down the hill, Shuja stopped and pointed ahead, toward the tip of the promontory.

"See," she said. "Var comes. And Net and Yova and Kern. They have salt. This is good."

Mana looked. The haze that covered the reedbeds all day was starting to turn golden as the sun moved toward its setting. Four weary people, each with two heavy gourds slung from their shoulders, had just emerged from it and were starting to climb toward the camp. Others had seen them too. She heard shouts from down the hill to her left, and everyone came running up from the fishing holes to greet the expedition.

By now they'd caught and found plenty of food, and down in the marsh the insects were always worst in the evening, so they built up the fire and prepared their meal while they caught up with each other's news. Po had caught three fish, which he shared with Mana. They were all smaller than the one she'd given away, but she didn't tell him.

At sunset, while they were still eating, the stranger woman gave a loud, wailing cry and began to tear with her nails at her face and chest, until the blood came. Mana didn't need to look to know that the man was dead.

At first the woman wouldn't let anyone touch him, but after a while they insisted. They were certainly not going to sleep with a dead man near them. A body might attract demons, come to eat the spirit that was still tied to it. Some of them held the woman while the others carried the corpse well up the hillside and piled rocks around and over it, and then in the last light the women did the death dance for the stranger, to set his spirit free, while his woman kneeled wailing at the foot of the pile.

Mana was too young to join in the dance. The stranger had let her take charge of her baby while she mourned for her man, and now Mana was sitting behind the line of women, with the little boy asleep in her arms, when she saw Noli break from the stamping rhythm, stiffen and sway. Bodu, beside her, caught and held her. Tinu took little Amola from her. The rest of the women stilled. The men stopped their slow handclap and their groaning chant. Last of all the stranger woman looked up and fell silent, staring bewildered as the voice of Moonhawk came slowly from between Noli's lips, deep and soft, but filling the long hillside with its sound.

"Blood falls," said the voice. "Men follow."

Noli's head dropped and her knees buckled, but Bodu and Tinu held her steady until she shook herself and snorted and looked around her. She murmured to Tinu and took the baby back. They all stared questioningly at each other. For a while no one said anything.

Mana could feel their fear and uncertainty. She knew they were all thinking the same thing. Moonhawk's brief message was frighteningly clear. *Blood falls.* The stranger man's wound had been oozing when Mana had first seen him. It must have dripped all the way as he had fled from his enemies, and had opened again and left a still clearer trail as he'd been carried to camp. *Men follow.* Not just a single enemy, then. At least two, perhaps several.

"Do they follow this trail in the dark?" said Var. "Do they smell it?"

"I say they do not," said Kern, who was the best tracker among them. "I say they wait. Tomorrow it is light. Then they come."

"How many men," asked Chogi. "Can Noli tell?"

"I do not see them," muttered Noli. "They are hunters, fierce, fierce."

Murmurs broke out. Mana saw Noli hold up her hand, but she seemed to be too dazed from Moonhawk's visitation to assert herself. Bodu had seen the movement, though, and called out, "Wait. Noli tells more."

Everyone fell silent again, straining to hear. This time Noli's voice was dreamy and very quiet, but her own.

"I was a child," she said. "We laired at Dead Trees Valley. I dreamed. Men came, fierce, fierce. They killed our men. They took our women. This was my dream. Moonhawk sent it. It was a true dream. These men came."

Everyone knew what she was talking about, though Mana herself had been only a small one when it had happened and couldn't remember it, except sometimes at the shadowy edges of a nightmare. The eight Kins had been living peaceably in the Old Good Places, as they'd done ever since the time of the Oldtales, when a horde of murdering strangers had burst upon them, killing all the males they could, and taking the women for themselves.

Only the Moonhawk Kin had had any warning, because of Noli's dream, but then they hadn't believed her.

Now they did. There was a horrified silence before Chogi asked the question in everyone's mind.

"These are the same men?"

Noli hesitated.

"I do not know," she muttered. "I think…I think they are others."

Tun took charge.

"Hear me," he said. "We keep watch tonight, by three and by three. We hide the fire. Tomorrow we wake in the dark. We are ready. We set lookouts. They see who comes, how many. Few men, we meet them. They see we are more. They go away. Many men, we go into the marsh. We know the paths. They do not. Is this good?"

There were mutters of agreement, and they went back down to the camp, deciding as they went who should do what and how they should confront the strangers if it came to that.

Only the dead man's woman stayed mourning on the hillside. In the middle of the night she crept into the camp. By then her baby was restless and whimpering, but she took him and suckled him for a while, and then lay down at Mana's side and slept.

Huddled in her lookout, almost at the ridge that ran along the top of the promontory, Mana waited for Po's signal. He was farther along the hillside, at a point from which he could see a long way north. The hunters were sure to be following the bloodtrail. Very early that morning Kern had tracked it as far as the point at which Po would first see them appear, so he knew exactly where to look. Mana couldn't see him yet, as he was below the skyline on the far side of a low spur.

Slowly the shadows of the rocks shifted as time dragged past. Around midmorning Po suddenly appeared, crawling beween two boulders. As soon as he was below the skyline again, he stood and raised both arms. Mana did the same, to show she had seen the signal. Now Po lowered his right arm and raised it again, once, twice, three times, four....

Four hunters only. She sighed with relief as she answered the signal, then moved to where she could pass the news on to the camp. Suth waved back, turned and spoke to the people at the camp, waited for an answer and turned back to her. He raised both hands and pushed them toward her.

Stay there.

Since the hunters were few, the adults of the Kin would wait at the camp and face them. Mana waved and passed the order back to Po, who answered and crawled out of sight. Then she waited, dry mouthed, heart hammering, her eyes on the point where the bloodtrail crossed Po's spur, a long way down from his lookout.

Below her the hillside seemed empty. Suth had vanished. The marsh was hidden under its usual haze. Somewhere out there, a safe distance along the winding paths, the mothers were waiting with the babies and small ones. Everyone else was concealed among the boulders around the camp.

The hunters came much sooner than she'd expected, slinking across the skyline. One, two, three, four, swift and stealthy, pausing, peering ahead, and then darting on to the next piece of cover. They weren't hiding for fear of meeting some enemy, only because they didn't want to alarm their prey. Every now and then their leader would crouch, point and peer for a moment at something on the ground. Mana knew what he'd found—another speck of the bloodtrail. It didn't take them long to reach the hollow where Mana had first discovered the strangers.

They crouched at its edge for a moment and slipped down out of sight. Mana ducked behind a boulder and signaled to the camp. Suth didn't risk an answer, but she was confident he'd seen her. She returned to her watch.

The hunters were out of sight for a while. They would be reading the signs that Kern had found—the man had lain here and bled, the woman had kneeled here, the child had pissed here, chewed fishbones had been spat out here. Then others had come. The man had been helped, lifted. His wound had opened....

Now she saw them again, but this time it was only a single head peering over the rim of the hollow, studying the hillside ahead. Yes, they had read the signs well, so they knew they had more than one woman and a wounded man to deal with.

All four came out of the hollow and moved on, crouching and darting, taking more trouble to hide but moving just as confidently as before. As they passed below her, Mana got her first clear view of them. They were different from any people she knew, with long, thin arms and legs, and skins as dark as her own, but not her deep clear brown. Theirs was grayer, with a faint purple tinge beneath the surface. They wore belts with one or two strange pale gourds slung from them, and carried pointed sticks, longer than ordinary digging sticks but shorter and stouter than the fishing stick Mana had been using yesterday.

Every now and then one of them would freeze and stare, and Mana would freeze with him and hold her breath, sure that this time as the fierce gaze swept across the slope he would notice the glisten of an eye behind the crack between two boulders. It was hard not to sigh with relief as the gaze moved past her and on.

Despite these pauses the men covered the ground quickly. Soon they had almost reached the camp. When they were still about ten and ten paces away from it, Tun, Suth, Var, and Kern, with their digging sticks in their hands, rose from behind rocks. Tun took a pace forward with his left hand raised in greeting and his hair peaceably still.

The strangers scarcely hesitated. Instantly their hair bushed out. They gave a sharp, barking shout and charged. The four Kin shouted in answer and raised their digging sticks. Mana saw Kern, nearest her, parry a thrust, and then the rest of the Kin rose from their hiding places and rushed to join the scuffle. Their cries echoed along the hillside, savage and furious. One of the strangers broke from the throng and raced away. Nobody but Mana saw him go. She stood up, pointed, and yelled, but her voice was lost in the uproar. By the time the fighting stopped, he was well along the slope.

She yelled again. Heads turned. She pointed. Net and Tor raced off after the man, but he had too great a start and they soon gave up. Mana turned back to the others. She could see one body—no, two—lying on the ground, partly hidden by people's legs. Somebody was sitting on a rock, nursing a wounded arm. Chogi was looking at somebody's hurt head. Suth waved at Mana and pointed toward Po's lookout, then waved again, beckoning. Mana passed the message on to Po and ran down the hill.

It was Tun whose arm was wounded, a deep gash from a thrust in that first attack. Yova's eye was swollen shut. She'd been hit by the butt of somebody's digging stick as he'd drawn it back to strike. Shuddering, Mana looked at the bodies, three of them, the third one down in the hollow by the fire. They all belonged to the strangers. The two she'd first seen lay facedown, but the third, bloody and battered, stared blindly at the sky. At his side lay the thing that had hung from his belt. It wasn't any kind of gourd. It was a human skull.

Appalled, terrified, Mana turned away. Suth was at her side, staring down at the dead man and the dreadful thing beside him. She clung to him and buried her face in his side, while he put his arm around her and held her.

"This is demon stuff," he muttered.

Oldtale
The Rage of Roh

Dop fought with Gul. Gul won. Fat Pig and Snake saw this.

Snake said, "See. My man Gul is better."

Fat Pig said, "The sun shone in Dop's eyes."

Snake said, "Gul made it so. He was clever."

He laughed. He went back to the Mountain, the Mountain above Odutu.

Fat Pig was angry. He went to Dop. He breathed on him. He healed his wounds. He filled him with strength.

Still Dop slept. Fat Pig sent him a dream. In the dream he spoke to him. He said, "Dop, my piglet, you are dishonored by Gul. He took your dilli buck. Now he boasts to his Kin. He says, *I fought with Dop. I beat him. He was grass before my blows.* Dop, what do you say to my Kin? What boast do you make?"

Dop woke. He remembered the fight

with Gul. He looked, and saw the dilli buck was gone. He was filled with fresh rage.

He journeyed to Sam-Sam, to the cliff of caves. Fat Pig camped there. Their leader was Roh. He was Dop's father. He was old.

Dop stood before him. He said "Roh, my father, I am dishonored."

Roh said, "Dop, my son, who dishonors you?"

Dop said, "Gul dishonors me, of the Kin of Snake. It happened thus and thus." And he told of the fight.

Roh was foolish. He did not say in his heart, *My son fought all day with Dop. I see his wounds. They are healed. This is First One stuff.* He did not think. He was filled with rage. It was like this:

See Sometimes River. The bed is empty. It is dry rocks. Deer drink at the pools. Now the flood comes. It is a hill of water. It rushes through the bed of the river. The deer flee. They are swift, but the water is swifter. It sweeps them away. They are gone. The river is filled with water. It roars.

Such was the rage of Roh.

He called the men of Fat Pig about him. He spoke fierce words. He filled the men with rage. He said, "Where do Snake camp?"

They answered, "Roh, Snake camp at Egg Hills. It is their Place. It is not ours. We do not go there."

Roh said, "Now you go to Egg Hills. You lie in wait for a man of Snake. You take vengeance on him for the dishonor of Dop."

The men of Fat Pig put food in their gourds. They sharpened their digging sticks. They set out for Egg Hills.

3

Nobody was willing to stay near the dead men, let alone touch them. Without any more discussion they moved away from the camp, while Nar went up the hill to keep lookout and Po ran down to the marsh to fetch the mothers and children.

Still staying close to Suth, Mana listened to the talk. Every so often another fit of shuddering welled up inside her from the memory of what she'd seen.

"Are these men?" said Kern. "Are they people? Are they demons?"

"I say they are people," said Var. "Their First One is a demon."

"Mana found a man," said Tun. "Four hunted him. We kill three. One runs. Now does he bring others?"

"I say this," said Chogi. "Noli is right. Moonhawk showed her. We were in the Old Good Places. Strangers came. They gave no warning. They killed men. They took women. These are like those."

Mana heard mutters of anger at the memory. It was no wonder that the normally peaceful Kin had fought so fiercely.

"Those others had words," said Kern. "Do these? This man—he runs. He finds his others—other demon men. He says to them, *This happened.* How does he say this?"

"Kern, I do not know," said Chogi. "I say they come."

"Those other strangers were many, too many," said Var. "We could not fight them. These four carried sharp sticks. They were not digging sticks. They were not fishing sticks. I say they were fighting sticks. These are fighters, they are people-killers. Soon many come. We cannot fight them."

For once nobody laughed at Var for his gloomy forebodings. What he said was only too likely to be true. The four strangers hadn't been hunting the wounded man for vengeance—or for any reason that the Kin could understand. They had hunted him because they were killers. The skulls at their belts said that.

"Hear me," said Tun decisively. "I say this. We do not stay here. This is a demon place."

Nobody argued. With those dead men in and around the camp, how could it be anything else?

"We do not sleep in the marsh," Tun went on. "There is sickness. We do not go north. These men come from there. It is dangerous, dangerous. We go to the other side of this hill, far and far. We walk on hard rock. Our feet are careful. We leave no trail."

"Tun," said Kern. "The reeds there are dry. They are dead. They have no fish."

"Kern, you are right," said Tun. "We make paths in those reeds. We hide our paths. Out beyond is water. We fish there. All the time we keep watch on the hill. These demon men come. Our watchers see them. We hide in the reeds. Perhaps they find our paths. We make the paths narrow. These men come by one and by one. We fight them by one and by one. We lie in wait. For them it is dangerous, dangerous. Perhaps they do not come in the reeds. They are afraid.

"Hear me again. This is difficult. It is dangerous. It is not good. But what other thing do we do? Other things are worse."

They discussed the plan for a while. Nobody liked it, but as Tun had said, what else was there to do?

"I have a bad thought," said Var. Again, nobody laughed at him. "The rains go. Soon is west wind time. These men stand on the hill. Does the wind blow away the haze? Do the men see our paths?"

"Suth, what is this?" whispered Mana, puzzled and anxious. She didn't clearly remember when the rainy season had been a regular thing. Rapidly Suth explained that after the rains had ended, a steady wind used to blow from the west. Var was suggesting that if that happened here, the demon men might be able to see far across the marshes and work out where the Kin were hiding.

By the time she listened again, Kern—always much more cheerful than Var—was reminding them that soon after they'd arrived on the promontory he had explored far up its western side, and found very little in the way of food.

"This man runs away," he said. "He finds his others. How long is this? One day, two? I do not know. He says, *Men and women are in that place. Come. We hunt them.* This is another day. They bring food. They come. They do not find us. They eat their food. They have no more. They find no food here. Do they know fishing? I say they do not. They go away. We come out of the marshes. We fish. We keep watch. We do not hide all the time. This is better."

The rest of them talked it over, sounding slightly more cheerful. Mana felt Suth pat her comfortingly on the shoulder.

"Mana, you fish at your fishing hole," he said. "Is this good?"

She took his hand and squeezed it, but she found herself imagining what it would be like to crouch at her fishing hole, still and tense, waiting for a fish to come sidling into the open, but all the time wondering if one of the demon men had slipped unnoticed past the lookouts and was creeping along the path behind her. Another fit of shuddering shook her.

Suth kneeled and took her by the shoulders and looked her in the eyes.

"You are afraid?" he asked gently.

"They are demons," she muttered.

"Mana, you are Moonhawk," he said. "We are brave. We are clever. We are strong. Moonhawk helps us. These men are not demons. They are people. They say in their hearts, *All are afraid of us. All run before us.* But Moonhawk are not afraid. We do not run. First we hide. We make plans. We wait. We choose good times. We beat these men, these people-killers. We, Moonhawk, do this. You do it, Mana. You help."

She nodded and pulled herself together, squaring her shoulders and standing straight. Tun was right. It was going to be difficult and dangerous, but there was nothing else to do. And Suth was right too—Moonhawk could do it. But not if they let themselves be scared stupid.

Now the mothers came somberly up from the marsh with their small ones. Po had told them the news. As they climbed the hill they must have been having much the same discussions as those Mana had just heard. They stood and listened in silence while Tun explained his plan. His words meant nothing to the stranger woman, of course. She looked around, spotted Mana, and came and made questioning noises to her.

To save trying to explain with grunts and signs, Mana led her up the hill and across to a point from which they could look down onto the camp. The woman stared, gave a gasp of astonishment, thrust her child into Mana's arms and dashed off, not slowing her pace until she reached the spot. As soon as she'd regained her breath she kneeled by the two bodies that were lying face down and heaved them over onto their backs. Then she rose and stretched both arms to the sky and gave a great shout, like the scream of a furious beast.

She bent again and dragged the body by the fire up to the the other two and laid it beside them, then started to dance around them, alone on the rocky hillside, clapping her hands and singing at the top of her voice.

The others heard the glad and savage chant and came to see what it could mean. They watched the dance silently for a while.

"This is good," said Tun. "The demons do not come near her. She makes them afraid." He turned to Tinu. "Now Tinu fills the fire log."

Tinu scampered down the hill and did as Tun suggested. Mana wondered if perhaps Tinu wasn't as scared of demons as the rest of them. When she returned the stranger woman came with her, no longer the cowering, desperate creature she had been until now, but walking erect and smiling.

———

They climbed to the ridge, in a direction that took them farther to the north. Even the smallest children were careful to step where they would leave no footprints. Yova and Moru worked their way along the top to keep lookout, while the others moved down the other side of the promontory toward the western shore.

Below them lay another arm of the great reedbed they had come to know so well. Here the reeds grew not in good water, but out of an immense mudbank. It had dried out, and as a result large patches of reeds had died completely, leaving a confusion of dead stems. Though the rains had come and gone, even where the reeds still lived, the first green shoots were only just beginning to spear up through the brown, dry tangle.

It was midday by the time they reached the shore-line. Normally they would have rested through the heat, but most of the adults started at once on the slow and difficult task of cutting a hidden path into the reeds. Suth, though, said, "Come, Po. Come, Mana. We find lookout places," and led them up the hill.

Mana might not have spotted the feather if she hadn't been watching where she put her feet. She bent and eased it out from a cranny between two rocks—a single plume, of a dull bluish dark gray. When she held it at an angle to the sunlight the blueness seemed to rise to the surface and shimmer to and fro over the somber undercolor. She knew only one bird that had feathers like that.

"Suth, see what I find!" she said, and showed it to him.

He stopped and took it from her, making it do its trick with the sunlight.

"Moonhawk," he said. "Mana, you find a good sign." Smiling, he handed it back and they climbed on.

From the top of the ridge, Mana gazed down. Yes, she thought, Var had been right. The marsh haze was their friend. If an enemy stood where she was standing, he would see the reedbed clearly for the first few tens of paces and the people who were working there now, but beyond that everything would be vague brown dis-tances. Not even a broad trail would show up. But if the west wind came and brought clear air, then it would be far harder for the Kin to hide themselves.

They found Yova and Moru tucked down among the boulders on either side of the ridge, each with a clear view north along her part of the promontory.

"This is good," said Suth. "Now Mana and Po keep lookout. Yova and Moru go down. They cut reeds. I look for a thing."

So Po took over from Moru on the eastern side of the ridge, while Mana stayed on the western side. She settled and began to study the landscape to the north. The slope wasn't regular, but full of dips and rises. She looked for places where any attackers would need to cross some kind of ridge or spur, and she would have her best chances of spotting them. Below her Suth moved to and fro, searching the hillside. Mana had no idea what he wanted until he heaved up a flat slab of rock and staggered with it up the hill. He was gasping with the effort by the time he reached her.

He kneeled and propped the slab upright, just above the lookout. Now Mana saw that all its surface was covered with glittery little specks, which made it much paler than any of the other rocks around.

When Suth had recovered his breath, he said, "One watcher waits by the path into the reeds. He sees this rock. He says in his heart, *No enemy comes.*"

He laid the rock flat.

"The watcher does not see this rock," he said. "He says in his heart, *It is gone. An enemy comes.* He tells others. They hide. Is this good?"

Mana remembered how fast the demon men had covered the ground in their first attack. There wouldn't be time for the lookouts on the hill to run down to the shore and warn the others. Even to shout or to stand and wave might be dangerous. But...her heart tightened with renewed dread.

"But the watchers, Suth?" she whispered. "Where do they go?"

He nodded confidently.

"I find a place," he said.

Again he searched the slope, pausing often to gaze north and crouching low whenever he crossed open ground. Mana returned to her watch, but as she scanned the hillside her mind kept telling her, *This is danger. All the time it is danger. All the time we move like Suth. We watch. We run. We hide. We are afraid.*

Suth didn't find what he wanted in front of her or below her, so he moved out of sight behind her, and after a short while called softly to her to come. She did, moving as he had moved, and found him squatting beside a large slab a little way down the hill, doing something with a few smaller rocks at its lower end. As she kneeled beside him, he lifted one of them away and showed her a narrow opening beneath the slab.

"I am too big," he said. "Can you go under this rock? Take my digging stick. Look for scorpions."

Cautiously Mana wormed her head and shoulders into the slot and prodded around with the digging stick. When her eyes were used to the dimness she could see that farther in, the space widened enough for her to wriggle through and squirm around until she could see out into daylight.

"This is good," said Suth. "See. Take this."

He passed one rock in to Mana and placed the others across the opening, leaving a narrow gap, then removed the rocks and made her practice reaching out and dragging them back into place, before fitting the one he'd given her into the final gap. Next he fetched Po and tested whether there was room for him to fit in beside Mana. There was, just, but Po had to work his way in feetfirst and then almost wrench his chest through the slot. When Suth was satisfied he let them come out.

"Suth," said Po. "This place is small. Does Yova go in there? Does Moru?"

"Po, they do not," Suth answered. "Few can keep lookout. Tinu and Shuja—they are small. You, Po, and Mana. That is all. Now, Po, you go back to your place. I bring Tinu and Shuja. I show them. Mana, wait."

So she crouched beside him on the roasting hillside until Po was out of sight. Then he looked her in the eyes and said, "Mana, you do this? You are not afraid?"

She swallowed. The slot beneath the rock looked like the mouth of a burrow. Mana had many times dug small animals out of their burrows, listening eagerly to their terrifed squeakings as she came nearer to their nest. Now it would be her and Po in the burrow. She knew that Suth must have guessed what she was thinking, or he wouldn't have asked. She looked down at her hand and realized that she was still grasping the moonhawk feather.

"Yes, Suth, I do this," she answered.

She watched him stand and use the sole of his foot to blur away any betraying scrape marks that the rocks might have left as they were dragged in and out. Then she crept back to her lookout while he made his way down to the marsh.

For the first time ever that Mana could remember, they made no camp that night. There was no cheerful fire. The workers had cut an open circle at the far end of the path they had made into the marsh, and floored it with mud and built their fire out there, banking it around with more mud and leaving two small openings above and below for air, so that there would still be embers hot enough in the morning to start a fresh fire. Like that, it was invisible from the shore and there was no danger of any spark setting light to the great reedbed on which their safety depended.

The reedbed was now their home. The hillside was

only a place where they could sleep, away from the nighttime sickness of the marsh. Every evening from now on they would choose a different place on the hillside, and try to leave no trace that they had been there. Anyone old enough to control themselves must make dung and pass water out among the reeds, and the mothers must clean up as best they could after their babies.

They were settling down among the unfamiliar rocks when Mana heard someone say, "Be quiet. Listen."

Her heart stood still. Had the speaker heard a footfall or the click of a pebble dislodged as unseen figures crept toward them?

No. From north along the promontory came a high, harsh shriek, thrice repeated, *yeek-yeek-yeek*, then a pause and the call again, and yet again. It was the cry of a moonhawk leaving its nest at nightfall to hunt among the rocks for its prey, the shy little scurriers that came out of their burrows only in the dark.

"She is here," someone whispered. "She is with us. This is a Moonhawk place."

Mana knew she was not the only one to feel comforted.

Oldtale

The War Oath

The men of Snake said, "Today we hunt."

Jad was among them. His mate was Meena, from Little Bat. They were new mated. They were happy, happy. All saw their love. It was like this:

See this man. He says in his heart, *Now I make a cutter.* He chooses a good rock. He strikes it thus, and thus. His aim is true. The chips fly from the rock. The edge is sharp, strong, a clean curve. He holds the cutter in his palm. His fingers close around it. Cutter and hand, they are one thing. He is glad, glad.

Such was the love of Jad for Meena and of Meena for Jad.

Meena said, "Jad, I come with you? I see you hunt?"

Jad asked the men. They laughed. They said, "Let her come."

They came to the deer pastures. They

spread apart. Jad said to Meena, "Come behind me, ten paces. Do not be seen."

The men of Fat Pig lay in wait. Mott was among them. Rage was in his heart. Jad came close. Mott gave no warning. He sprang out upon Jad. He struck him with his digging stick, on the side of the neck. Jad fell. Blood flowed. Mott raised his digging stick for another blow.

Meena saw this. She ran between the men. Mott did not see, he did not think, his rage filled him. He struck again. His digging stick was sharp, it was heavy. It hit Meena between the breasts. It broke through her ribs. It entered her heart. She fell on Jad's body. They were dead.

Now the rage left Mott. He saw Jad's body and Meena's. He did not rejoice. He said in his heart, *I have done this thing. It is bad, bad.* He dragged the bodies under bushes. He ran from that place.

The men of Fat Pig saw him. They said, "Mott runs. We run also."

So they fled.

The men of Snake rejoiced. They said, "Fat Pig are weak, they are cowards. We are brave and strong. But where is Jad? Where is Meena?"

They searched. They found the bodies of Jad and of Meena. The men were filled with rage.

Ziul was Jad's brother. He said, "Fat Pig did this thing. Now we, Snake, take vengeance. Come."

They pursued the men of Fat Pig. They came to Sam-Sam, to the cliff of caves. The men of Fat Pig met them. Again they fought. The men of Snake fought better. They struck fierce blows. They killed two. The men of Fat Pig fled.

The men of Snake rejoiced. They said, "We have vengeance for Jad."

But Ziul said, "It is not enough. We do not have vengeance for Meena."

He entered the caves. He found Dilu, Tong's mate. She hid there. She was from Ant Mother. Ziul struck her. She died.

Ziul returned to the men of Snake. He said, "Rejoice. I have vengeance for Meena."

The men of Snake did not answer. Shame was in their hearts. They went home.

The men of Fat Pig said, "We take vengeance for Dilu. But the men of Snake are too strong. We need friends."

They sent to Ant Mother and to Weaver and to Parrot.

To Ant Mother they said, "Take vengeance on Snake for Dilu, who was your daughter."

To Weaver they said, "Sam-Sam is your Place. There Snake killed Dilu, a woman. You are dishonored."

To Parrot they said, "You fought Moonhawk in our father's time. We helped you. Now help us."

The men of Snake said, "Fat Pig send to their friends. They take vengeance on us for Dilu. Let us send also, to Little Bat, and to Crocodile and to Moonhawk."

To Little Bat they said, "Fat Pig killed Meena, who was your daughter. Take vengeance upon them."

To Crocodile they said, "Ant Mother fights against us. Yellowspring is their Place. You want it. Now help us. We beat them. You take Yellowspring. It is yours."

To Moonhawk they said, "Parrot fights against us. You have blood debts to settle. Help us. We help you."

The Kins spoke among themselves. Some men did not want this. They said, "Mott killed, and Ziul. Let Mott be given to Snake. Let them kill him. Let Ziul be given to Fat Pig. Let them kill him. It is finished."

These men were few.

Other men said, "Let us fight. Let us go to Odutu. Let us swear the War Oath."

These men were many.

So all gathered at Odutu. First came Snake and Fat Pig. They laid their hands upon the rock. They swore the War Oath. The others watched. They said, "Tomorrow we too swear. It is war."

4

For ten and two more long days they saw no sign of the murderous strangers. There were two lookout places, one on either side of the ridge, each with its own signal stone. Morning after morning, Mana crouched at one of them, scanning the now familiar hillside for the faintest flicker of movement. Her tension never lessened. She knew in her heart the enemy would be back in the end, and if they weren't spotted far off there would be no time for everyone to hide, and then there would be fighting and slaughter. However bravely the Kin fought, if the attackers came in too great numbers, then Moonhawk and all the other Kins would be gone for ever. The demon men would kill all the males— Tun, Suth, Tor, Po, even little Ogad—while the women and girls—Yova and Noli, Bodu, Tinu, Mana herself, all of them—would be taken away to become the mates of these demon men and bear their demon children.

Perhaps Moonhawk would send a warning, as she'd done before. Perhaps not. You could never tell with First Ones.

So Mana watched unwavering, with Po on the other side of the ridge, doing the same. They changed places, so that they didn't become stale with watching the same hillside all the time. They were alone.

If Mana was on the western side and looked down to the marsh, she could see nothing of her friends. But she knew they were there, cutting the main path farther and farther across the mudbank, or making side paths and blind alleys to confuse anyone who didn't know the way. Out there, somewhere, the precious fire was burning, but she could see no sign of it through the haze, and smelled no whiff of smoke.

If she was on the other side and looked down she would see a few people foraging along the shoreline or coming or going along one of the paths that led to a fishing hole. If an attack came while they were out, there would be no time for them to climb and cross the ridge and reach the safety of their main hideout in the reeds. So they had cut another path here, with a hidden entrance and its own maze of traps and side turnings. If danger threatened they could hide there. At least two of the men always stood by to defend the second path if they had to.

Like everything else, this was dangerous, but they were forced to take the risk because there was so little food of any kind on the western shore, and their main path had not yet reached the far side of the great mudbank, where there was clear water and they could fish.

At midday Tinu and Shuja would come stealthily up from the western marsh to take over lookout, and Mana and Po, watching every step they took, would creep back down the hill. By then Mana's head would throb and her eyes would be sore with endlessly gazing at the rock-strewn slope lit by the glaring sun.

Somebody was always down at the shore, waiting for the moment that the pale rock by the lookout vanished, signaling that the enemy had been seen. Po and Mana greeted the watcher and then, at a particular point in the great tangle of reeds along the shoreline, lifted a broken mass of stems and crawled into the gap beneath them, and on along a twisting tunnel, until they reached the main path. There were three such entrances, so that everyone out in the open could get quickly into cover.

The path itself twisted to and fro to make it harder to see from the hillside. Twice in that first stretch Po and Mana stopped and, instead of going straight on—those were blind alleys—slipped between reedstems to where the real path continued beyond.

On the third day, just beyond the second of these places, they found Net and Var toiling away, with sweat streaming from their bodies in the steamy heat. They had cleared the cut reeds from the floor of the path and were using their digging sticks to loosen the mud beneath.

"Var, what do you do?" asked Po.

"We make a trap," said Var. "It is Tinu's thought. See, we make the mud soft…" He stepped onto the patch he had been working on. Immediately his leg started to sink.

"Soon we finish," he went on. "We put the reeds back. We can walk on them. This is safe. But demon men come. They find our path. We run. We cross here. Then we take reeds away. We wait this side. Demon men come. They walk on the mud. They sink. We fight them with digging sticks. They are in the mud. They cannot fight well. This is good for us."

The men went back to their work, and Po and Mana moved on.

By now the path had reached what had once been an island, with trees and bushes growing on it. Most of these had died in the drought, so there was good fuel for a fire, as well as a safer place for it to burn without setting fire to the whole vast reedbed.

This was now their daytime lair. By the time Po and Mana reached it, most of the others would have gathered there for their midday rest and meal, but as soon as they'd finished eating they all went back to work. Mana helped with whatever needed doing—collecting fuel, preparing food, laying and firming reeds in the pathways, or searching for birds' nests and for insect bait for fishing. As the sun dipped toward the horizon everyone except the lookouts gathered again on the island for their evening meal.

This was scanty for the first few days, since most of the Kin were either on watch or working desperately to make their hideout secure, and to drive the path to the far side of the mudbank, where they could fish in safety. This left only a few of them to fish among the eastern reeds and forage along that shore. But they ate what they had and were glad of it.

Then, as dusk fell, they came ashore moving as carefully as ever, and climbed to wherever Tun had chosen for them to lair. Mana at first dreaded these times, and knew that she was not the only one. The moon was small, and the nights were very dark. The dark belonged to the demons. Everyone knew that. That was why, however hot the season and whether or not there was food to cook, when the Kin made a fresh camp the first thing they always did was to light a fire, so that they could sleep in its friendly glow and know that the demons would be afraid to come too near.

But they could have no fire now, with its flame farseen in the night and its betraying ash left on this hillside in the morning. They were forced to sleep in the dark, and from time to time Mana would wake, tense with terror, and hear a small one whimper or an adult sigh, and know that someone else was awake too, and as afraid as she was.

But then, from north along the promontory, she would hear one of the moonhawks call. These were just a pair of ordinary moonhawks, each hunting in turn, while the other one fed the chicks with what it had just caught, but hearing that cry Mana would sense that Moonhawk herself was hovering near her in the dark, ready to warn, ready to guard the last of her Kin. Then Mana would master her fear and sleep again.

———

The maze of paths and traps was almost finished. The moon grew half large, and still there was no sign of the demon men. Mana heard the adults discussing whether they were going to come back at all. Var, of course, was sure that they would, and Kern just as sure they wouldn't. The others' opinions were in between.

"Hear me," said Tun at last. "They come, they do not come, who knows? But we say in our hearts, *They come*. This is best. Every day we are careful, careful. The moon grows big. It grows small again. Then we decide. I, Tun, say this."

So they didn't relax their watch but went about their business as if an attack might come that very day. Though they had reached the farther side of the mud-bank, the fishing there turned out to be disappointing, so several of the Kin still returned to their old fish holes on the eastern side. When there was nothing more for her to do around the island lair, Mana asked Suth if she could go and join them after she'd finished her stint on lookout.

She caught nothing on her first afternoon, but two nice little fish on the second. On the third afternoon the tiddlers had found the bait and started to feed, and she was waiting eagerly for something larger to nose into view, when she heard from the shoreline the whistling call of a small brown bird.

Mana laid her fishing stick down and waited, holding her breath. The bird had been common in the New Good Places on the southern side of the marsh, but nobody had seen it here. That was why they had chosen its call as a signal.

Again the bird called, but this time, listening for it, she could tell that it wasn't a real bird. Kern, on guard at the entrance to the hidden path, had seen the signal stone by the eastern lookout disappear and had given the danger signal. The watcher there had seen someone or something approaching from the north.

Mana let out her breath and rose with her heart pounding. She couldn't stay here. The entrance to her fishing hole was obvious from the shore. She picked up her gourd and fishing stick, checked quickly to see that there was no other trace of her presence, and ran back down the short path. Crouching low, she scuttled along the shore to where Kern was waiting.

"Good," he said. "Soon Moru comes. Then all are in."

He lifted a stack of reedstems and she crawled through. Just as on the other side, there was a tunnel before the path began, and a little way beyond it a trap like the one she'd seen Var and Net making. Tun was there, and the stranger woman with her child on her hip. (Noli had given them names: Ridi and Ovoth. As soon as Ridi had worked out that Tun was leader, she had simply attached herself to him and went everywhere he went.)

Mana had crossed the trap and was about to run on when Tun said, "Wait. My arm is not good. Take reeds from the trap. Not all. Some. Moru comes soon, and Kern. Then take all, quick, quick. Show Ridi. Why does Moru not come?"

Mana had never heard Tun sound so anxious. She laid her gourd and stick on the path and signed to Ridi to put Ovoth down. While Tun stood guard on the far side of the trap, she gathered up an armful of loose reeds, passed them to Ridi, and gestured to her to carry them back along the path.

The reeds were laid crisscross in several layers. Beneath them was clear water. Mana stripped two layers away and tested the ones she'd left by walking on them. She could feel them quake beneath her.

"Tun, do I take enough?" she asked.

He looked over his shoulder.

"Take from that side," he said. "Leave those."

She did as he'd said and was about to ask him again when she heard shouts from the entrance to the path— men yelling in anger—and a moment later Moru came racing along the path toward them.

Tun stood aside to let her pass. Mana shouted to her to keep to her right as she crossed the trap, but Moru didn't hear and stepped on the weak part. Her foot went through and she started to fall, but Mana grabbed her outstretched arm and dragged her over.

Before Mana could follow, a demon man appeared at the bend of the path, with another behind him. The leading one saw Tun, raised his fighting stick, and rushed at him with a yell.

"Back!" shouted Tun.

Mana turned to run. Ridi, bending to pick up Ovoth, blocked her way. Mana looked back and saw that Tun had retreated to the near side of the trap and was standing with his hair bushed full out and his digging stick raised to strike.

The man rushed at Tun and launched himself into his thrust. His front foot landed, hard, on the trap and sank straight through. He stumbled and started to fall. His momentum carried the thrust past Tun's thigh and just missed Mana behind him. Ridi bent, grabbed the end of the fighting stick with her free hand, and wrenched, just as Tun's stick slammed down into the man's back.

He screamed and collapsed, but as he fell his free hand reached out and grasped Tun's ankle. Tun was already moving back for another blow. Suddenly unbalanced, he fell on top of Mana. She was beginning to struggle up as the second man rushed toward them.

Ridi was the only one still standing. The first man had let go of his stick as he fell, but she'd kept hold of it. The second man paused for an instant, judging his leap across the trap. In that instant Ridi managed to reverse the spear, and as he sprang she screamed and darted to meet him, jabbing forward two-handed with all her strength. He didn't seem to see her. All his attention was on Tun. In the middle of his leap he drove himself onto the sharpened point of the stick. It sank into his stomach, just below the ribcage.

Ridi was knocked over backward by the force of their meeting, but by now Mana was on her feet. Tun was still on the ground, trying to kick the first man's grip from his ankle. He had let go of his digging stick. His left arm, wounded in the earlier fight, was still almost useless. Mana saw the stick lying at her feet, snatched it up, took a pace forward and hammered down on the first man's head. He gave a deep grunt and let go of Tun's ankle. While Tun was getting to his feet she hammered twice more, to make sure. The last blow felt different. Something gave way beneath it. The man lay facedown in the water and didn't move.

The second man was kneeling on the edge of the trap where Mana had left the extra layers of reeds. The stick point was still in his stomach, and he was grinning taut-lipped, with all his teeth showing. He dragged the stick free and started to try to rise, blood streaming down his belly. Tun took the digging stick from Mana, aimed, and struck him savagely on the side of the neck, above the collarbone. Still grinning, he toppled sideways on top of the other man.

They stood side by side, panting, with the dead men at their feet.

"Mana, I thank. Ridi, I thank," said Tun. "I fear for Kern. Where is he?"

While Tun guarded the path Mana and Ridi rearranged the reeds over the trap so that they hid the water below but would collapse under any weight. Then they waited a long while, but no one else, friend or foe, appeared along the path.

"Go, Mana," said Tun. "Find others. Tell them our doing. Say, *Come. Make this trap strong.* I look for Kern."

Mana hurried away. She found Yova, Moru, Rana, and Galo waiting anxiously just beyond the first place where a false trail led on while the real path was hidden behind a screen of reeds. Moru was obviously very distressed, and the others had been trying to comfort her.

"Kern does not come?" she asked desperately.

Mana shook her head.

"It is my doing," Moru said, croaking with grief. "I did not hear the whistle birdcall. Kern came. He found me. We ran. The demon men saw us. They were five. They found the path. Kern said, *Run, Moru. I fight them.* I ran. Oh, Yova, Kern is dead."

It was true. When they returned to the trap they found Tun there, looking very grim. He had gone to the end of the path and seen blood on the trampled reeds at the entrance. The signal stone was not in its place by the lookout, so he'd known there must still be demon men around. There was nothing to do but leave the trap as it was and wait.

Toward evening the signal rock appeared, and at last everyone came out. They found Kern's body some way up the hill. They knew it had to be his from the color of the skin. Otherwise they wouldn't have known. The head was missing.

Tun stared grimly down at the body, saying nothing. The others waited. Mana started to sob and couldn't stop. Rana kneeled and held her. Dimly Mana was aware of Moru's voice, also racked with sobs, blaming herself over and over, and of the other women trying to comfort her, though they were weeping too.

At last Tun said, "We do not leave him here." So they lifted the battered body, two at the shoulders, two at the thighs, and Mana carrying the trailing feet, and with Tun leading, carried it up to the mound of rocks they had piled over the stranger man. They laid it down beside the mound and heaped more rocks over it.

It was exhausting labor, but it felt to Mana that at least she was doing all she could for Kern, and this seemed to ease her grief. Before they had finished, some of the others came up from the western marsh. They had seen the signal stone on their side reappear, so they knew the danger was over and had come to see what had happened.

In the late dusk they crossed the ridge and found the rest of the Kin already assembling on the hillside. They had brought food with them, but Mana was unable to eat. Someone had already run down to the marsh with the news of the attack, so instead of settling down to sleep they sat and talked it over.

The half-moon was rising, but not yet above the

ridge, so this slope was still in deep darkness. Only now, sitting there, unable to see the faces but listening to the well-known, troubled voices, did Mana begin to feel something deep inside her that she hadn't before realized was there.

In the terror of the sudden attack, that had been all she had felt—terror, almost drowning her wits, spurring her to run, and then to fight. After that came the immense relief of victory, and then the long anxiety of wondering what had happened to Kern, and the horror and grief of the answer.

But now, as she sat and gazed unseeing over the vague distances of the moonlit marsh, a different thought came to her.

I have killed people.

Yes. The attackers had been demon people, but that didn't make them any less people. Mana wasn't sorry for what she had done. If she hadn't done it, perhaps Tun would be dead, and little Ovoth too, and she and Ridi and Yova and the other women who had been there would be being herded away to the north by their savage captors. She had had to kill the man. She was sure of that.

But despite that, everything had changed, and Mana herself would never be the same again.

She had killed people.

At last the moon crossed the ridge, and suddenly the whole slope was bathed in pale light, mottled by the dense black shadows thrown by the rocks. Tun rose.

"Hear me," he said. "We do no death dance for Kern. The demon men take his head. They take his spirit. He is not here. I say again, we do no death dance for Kern. We do this. Come."

He led the way to a large boulder. He waited for the

rest of them to gather around, and then reached up and laid his dark hand against the paler stone.

"This rock is Odutu," he said in a low, clear voice. "Odutu below the Mountain. On Odutu I say this. *These men kill Kern. He is Moonhawk. They take his head. For this I kill them, all, all. Not one lives. I, Tun, do this. On Odutu I say these words.*"

One after another all the adults, women as well as men, came to the boulder and laid their hand against it and swore the same oath. Moru could scarcely get the words out, and she was not the only one.

As she finished, the triple call of a hunting moonhawk rang through the night stillness.

Oldtale

Black Antelope's Waking

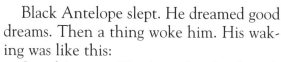

Black Antelope slept. He dreamed good dreams. Then a thing woke him. His waking was like this:

See this man. He sleeps by the fire. A log falls. Sparks jump out. One lands on the arm of the man. The pain is sharp, sharp. He wakes. He cries, "Oh!"

Such was Black Antelope's waking.

He said in his heart, *Men came to Odutu, Odutu below the Mountain. They laid their hands upon the Rock. They swore the War Oath.*

He looked down the Mountain. He saw the rock Odutu. He saw the Kins gathered about it. He breathed through his nostrils. His breath was thick mist.

The men slept. They woke. They were in thick mist. They could not see. They searched for the rock Odutu. They could not find it.

Black Antelope called the First Ones

about him. He said, "The Kins swear the War Oath. Why is this? Let Moonhawk speak."

Moonhawk said, "Parrot fights against Snake. My Kin has blood debts to settle with Parrot."

Black Antelope said, "Parrot, why does your Kin fight against Snake?"

Parrot said, "My Kin owes Fat Pig a debt. When they fought against Moonhawk, Fat Pig helped them."

Then Crocodile told the reason, and Weaver and Ant Mother and Little Bat.

Black Antelope looked at Snake. He said, "Your man Ziul killed a woman. Why is this?"

Snake said, "He sought vengeance for the death of Meena. Fat Pig's man Mott killed her."

Fat Pig said, "Mott was in rage, the rage of a hero. He did not see it was a woman."

Black Antelope said, "What made this rage?"

Fat Pig said, "My man Dop hunted. Snake's man Gul hunted. There was one dilli buck. Each man said it was his. They fought. Gul won by a trick. My man Dop was dishonored. My Kin was dishonored."

Weaver said, "Now I remember. Snake and Fat Pig drank stoneweed. There was much shouting. Each said his man was better. The men were Dop and Gul."

Black Antelope said, "Is this the seed of it?"

Fat Pig and Snake were filled with shame. They hid their heads.

Black Antelope spoke to the First Ones. He said, "You six, go now to your Kins. They did not swear the War Oath. Speak in their hearts. Say to them, *This is folly*. Send them back to their own Places."

They went down the Mountain, those six. They spoke in the hearts of their Kins. It was done.

Black Antelope spoke to Snake and to Fat Pig. He said, "This folly is your folly. You must undo it."

They said, "We go now to our Kins. We say to them, *Unswear your War Oath*."

He said, "This is not enough. On Odutu they swore, Odutu below the Mountain. How must they unswear? In their own hearts they must do it, not from your telling. I know you two. You say in your hearts, *I cheat Black Antelope. My Kin is mine. I wish a thing, they do it.* So now I do this to you."

He put his nose against theirs. He breathed in. He drew their powers out of them. Fat Pig was Fat Pig no more. He was a pig of the reedbeds. He was fat.

Snake was Snake no more. He was a tree serpent, green and black. He was long.

They said, "Our powers are gone. Our Kins do not hear our words. We cannot speak to them."

Black Antelope said, "I give you this. Go to your Kins. One sees you first. That one hears your words, that one only. Now go."

5

They woke with the first light. As they searched the hillside for any traces of their stay, Mana could hear a different note in their voices. Anger, as well as fear. She felt the difference in herself. The fear itself was different too, like a different taste in the mouth, not thin and acid as before, but rounder and stronger. The taste of something she could feed on, use.

She thought about it later that morning, crouching in her lookout, and decided that if it were possible she would rather have the old fear back. Of course, if she needed to, she would again fight as fiercely as any of the adults who had sworn the oath. If the chance came to kill another of the demon men she would seize it. Horrible, but she had no choice. Why should she alone be spared the horror?

But there had been a different Mana yesterday, one who had never killed people. That Mana had been happier, despite her fear.

She and Po watched all morning, but saw no sign of danger. There was no question now of fishing in the eastern marsh, with the path no longer hidden and the spirits of the dead men bringing demons to lurk among the reeds. So they went down the other side and out to the island and ate scraps for their midday meal. But Suth came in with the cheering news that the path had now reached a new area of water where the fishing was better, and several fish holes had already been cut. When Mana and Po had eaten they went out to see, and were allowed to fish at one of these. They took turns. Mana caught nothing, but Po speared a good fish, short but deep-bodied, and carried it back to the island in triumph.

Not far into the night, as she slept on the hillside, Mana was awakened by the moon rising above the ridge. It was now more than half full, its light even brighter and the shadows it cast even blacker than they had seemed the night before. The moonhawks were again busy, coming and going in quick succession as the stronger light made it easier for them to find their prey.

Someone close by was moaning in her sleep. The sound stopped, and Mana saw a dark figure—Noli—push herself up and stand with arms spread wide, facing the moon. The bottom half of her body was in shadow, but the top half was clear in the sharp, pale light. The voice of Moonhawk breathed in slow syllables into the silence.

"Big moon…Men…Bring Kern…"

Mana rose and crept to Noli's side, ready to ease her fall.

"Big moon…" sighed the voice again.

Noli shuddered. Mana put her arms around her. Noli's body went as rigid as a log, and then, just as quickly, slack. Mana was almost knocked over by the sudden weight, but she managed to lower her to the ground, still asleep but again moaning softly, while everyone else, wide awake now, sat up and wondered in whispers what the message could mean. It was a long time before any of them slept again.

The next morning went much the same as the day before. Mana and Po kept lookout and saw nothing.

But as they went down the hill at noon they felt a change. There was a wind blowing in their faces. The adults were already talking about it as they reached the island.

"I say this," said Var. "These demon men find no food here. They go back to their place, they get food, they bring it. This is two days. It is three. I do not know. Now west wind comes. The men stand on the hill. They look far. They see the marsh. Do they see our path? Our island? I say they do."

"Moonhawk says big moon," said Net. "Three days is not big moon."

"Hear me," said Suth. "I say this. Var is right. Net is right. Say in your hearts, *I am a demon man.* Now say, *Men, women are in this place. We are many. We hunt them. Where are they?* What do you do? I say first you come, few, few. You hide. You look this way, that way. You see the marsh. The mist is gone. You say, *They are there.* You search the rocks. You smell baby piss. You find people hair. You say, *They sleep here.* You say, *At night we come, at big moon. Moon is strong. We find these men, these women. They are asleep.* I think you do all this."

"Suth, you are right," said Chogi.

"This wind is bad, bad," said Var.

A slight movement caught Mana's eye. Tinu, sitting a few places to her left. She had reached across Bodu to touch Noli's wrist. Bodu shifted out of the way, and while the others continued to talk, Tinu squatted beside Noli and mumbled into her ear. Mana couldn't hear what Tinu was saying, but she could see how eagerly she struggled to get the words out through her twisted mouth.

After a while Noli signaled to Suth, who rose from

among the men on the far side of the fire and came around. Tinu shuffled back, and she and Suth crouched together, he listening and sometimes asking a question, Tinu mumbling excitedly away, scratching on the ground with a stick, rubbing the marks out, and drawing again.

Mana saw Nar watching them anxiously. Since he and Tinu had chosen each other, though they were not yet mates, he had been very protective of her. And Tinu had grown more confident, but still she would never dream of standing up in front of everyone and telling them some idea she had had, though they all would have been ready to listen.

Now the rest of them continued to argue about when and how the next attack would come, but somehow aimlessly, as they waited to hear what Tinu was telling Suth.

At last he moved back to his place among the men, but didn't sit down. He looked at Tun.

"Speak, Suth," said Tun. "We hear."

"Hear me," said Suth. "This is not my thought. It is Tinu's. I say it for her. Var is wrong. This wind is not bad. It is good."

Stage by stage he told them Tinu's terrifying plan.

They argued about it for a long while, some of them adding ideas and details, others making objections. Var kept saying how dangerous it was and how many things could go wrong. What if the wind died? What if the demon men realized it was a trap? What if only a few men came after all? What if…?

Every time he raised one of these doubts, Mana heard mutters of agreement.

"Hear me," said Chogi suddenly. "I remember this. There was a demon lion. The men made a trap. Noli was bait, and Po. We killed the demon lion. It was Tinu's thought. There was a demon crocodile. The women dug a trap. Nar was bait. We killed the demon crocodile. This also was Tinu's thought. Demon men came to the reedbed. Tun fought them, and Ridi and Mana. They killed them. At a trap they did this. It was Tinu's thought. Now I say this. We make a new trap. We are bait, we women, our men, our children. I say in my heart, *This is dangerous, dangerous. But it is Tinu's thought. It is good.*"

"Hear me," said Tun. "I say this. Var speaks well. Chogi speaks well. Who is right? I do not know. But I have another thought. It is this. I swore an oath. On Odutu I swore it, Odutu below the Mountain. In my oath I said, *I kill these demon men.* How do I do this? It is difficult, difficult. Tinu shows me the way. It is enough."

That settled it. Even Var stopped arguing. He too had sworn the Oath upon Odutu below the Mountain, and however dangerous the undertaking, that oath was binding. The risk had to be taken.

They started at once on the task, Tun assigning the different jobs that had to be done, mostly cutting a huge new curving path through the dried-out reedbed between the island and the shore, but also hollowing out crude fire logs from whatever they could find, and cutting extra traps along the main entrance path.

But of course they still needed to eat, so Mana was sent off to fish at one of the new holes. As she settled down beside the little patch of water she felt that she would never catch anything. All of her, body and spirit, seemed to be vibrating, silently buzzing, with a new mixture of excitement and hope and fear. At first the long, poised stillness needed for fishing seemed quite impossible, but soon she found that her feelings seemed to weave themselves together, telling her that what she was doing now, as well as what she was going to do, was all part of the plan. They were things within her power, not beyond her. If she did them right, the Kin would survive. If not, then not.

So focussed, she fished eagerly, passionately, all afternoon, and it seemed to her that her waiting was stiller than usual, her aim surer, her strike swifter. She made five strikes in all, and as the sun went down toward the west and the strange clean air glowed with gold light, she came back to the island with five good fish threaded on her stick.

For the next three days Mana saw very little of the work that everyone else was doing. In the mornings she kept lookout on the ridge, at midday she went back to the island and gobbled whatever food had been left over for her, and then went straight out to one of the fishing holes for the rest of the afternoon.

On the second day came a stroke of luck. Net, Yova, Nar, and Tinu, cutting the northern arm of the new path, reached the nesting area of a colony of marsh herons. Nar ran to fetch help, and while the adult birds circled, squawking furiously, the people robbed the nests of tens and tens of half-grown fledglings. There was a feast that evening on the island, and a change from the endless diet of fish. They left the marsh as darkness fell and climbed the hill with a strange, unreasonable feeling that all might yet be well.

That night, for the first time, they laired in the same place as the night before, a little way down the hill from the hiding place that Suth had found for the lookouts. When they left the next morning they made no attempt to conceal the fact that they'd been there—indeed, they deliberately left a few traces: a handprint in a soft patch, the spine of a small fish, a few strands of human hair.

Tinu's plan had several versions, depending on when and how the enemy chose to attack, and whether scouts would come first to spy on them. That would be best, for then the scouts would find a place where people had laired in the night, and the demon men would come and try to catch their prey sleeping unawares one night when the moon was big.

Noli was no help with any of this guesswork. Though Mana and many of the others had heard Moonhawk's message, Noli herself had no memory of it at all, only the shadowy knowledge that she had dreamed, and that Moonhawk had been there in her dream.

So each morning as Mana climbed the hill in the brief half-light, she told herself that today would be the day. She settled into her place as the sun rose and concentrated everything that was in her into a steadfast search of the hillside, working her way over it rock by rock by rock, making sure that she missed nothing at all, not the slightest movement or change.

Each day the wind blew ever more steadily, rattling the dead reedstems together and scouring the haze away, just as Var had said it would. By the third day Mana, slinking down the hill with Po after their stint on watch, could see the bright glimmer of water far out across the marsh, and beyond that other reedbeds and islands, stretching all the way to the western hills.

But to her relief, though she knew where the path was, she couldn't actually see it winding its way through the tangled reeds. The nearest island was the one where they laired, but there was no sign of the fire, or of people living there.

Oldtale

Siku

Fat Pig and Snake went down the Mountain. Black Antelope made himself invisible. He went with them. They did not see him.

They were afraid. They said in their hearts, *We have no powers. Men hunt us. They kill us. They roast our flesh on embers. They eat it. We are gone. This is bad, bad.*

Fat Pig said, "My Kin lair at Windy Cliff. They do not eat Pig. I go there. I hide in long grasses. I wait. I see Roh, who is leader. I show myself to him. He sees me first. He hears my words. This is good."

Fat Pig journeyed to Windy Cliff. Black Antelope went with him. Fat Pig did not see him.

———

Now Kin fought with Kin, Snake against Fat Pig. They raided, they lay in wait, they set traps. They struck fierce blows, they threw rocks, they bit with their teeth, blood flowed, men died. Those times were bad.

The men of Fat Pig said, "The rains are gone. Soon all the Kins go to Mambaga. The white-tail buck cross the river. The Kins hunt them. We do not fight at Mambaga. It is a Thing Not Done. But see, now Snake lair at Old Woman Creek. They go to Mambaga by way of Beehive Waterhole. We go now. We lie in wait for them there."

They sharpened their digging sticks. They set out. The women stayed. They were sad.

Siku was a child. She had no father, no mother. She foraged with the women. No one watched her.

She came to the cliff. A bloodberry vine grew there. It was like this:

See Gata the Beautiful. Her hair was long, long. It shone. It flowed down over her shoulders. Her skin was hidden.

So the bloodberry vine flowed down the cliff.

Siku saw good bloodberries. She said in her heart, *They are too high. The vine is weak. The women are heavy. They do not climb to them. But I am a child, light. I climb.*

She took hold of the vine. She climbed. The vine broke. She fell. She fell upon a soft thing. It was Fat Pig. He hid behind the vine.

Siku spoke as a child speaks, thus: "Pig, why do you hide? My Kin is Fat Pig. We do not eat pig."

Fat Pig did not answer. He said in his heart, *Must I speak to a child? Must she carry my words to my Kin? Who will hear me?"*

Siku said, "Oh, pig, I am sad, sad. Men lay in wait. They killed my father. I have no father. My mother grieved. She did not eat. A sickness took her. I have no mother."

Fat Pig said in his heart, *This is my doing.* He spoke. He said, "Siku, I hear you."

Siku said, "Oh, pig, you have words! How is this? Is it demon stuff?"

Fat Pig said, "Siku, it is not demon stuff. I am Fat Pig."

Siku kneeled down. She laid her forehead on the ground. She fluttered her fingers. She said, "Oh, Fat Pig, I am your piglet. The men go to Beehive Waterhole. They lie in wait for Snake. Say to them, *Do not do this.*"

Fat Pig said, "Siku, they do not hear me. Only you hear me."

Siku said, "Fat Pig, how is this?"

Fat Pig said, "Black Antelope made it so. I do not tell you more. It is my shame."

Siku said, "Fat Pig, this is not good. Our women said to the men, *Do not go.* The men said, *There is rage in our hearts. We go.* How do the men hear me, Siku? I am a child, a girl child."

Fat Pig thought. He said, "We find Snake. He is at Old Woman Creek."

Siku said, "That is far, too far."

Fat Pig said, "Climb on my back. I go quick."

Siku climbed on his back. All day he ran, and all night. Black Antelope went with them. They did not see him. They came to Old Woman Creek.

6

On the fourth morning demon men appeared again, soon after Mana had started her watch at the top of the western slope above the dried-out reedbed. So single-mindedly was she concentrating on searching the hillside before her that she almost missed Po's signal from the eastern side of the ridge.

Had she really heard it? The call of the whistle-bird, suddenly cut short? Or had she imagined it so strongly that the sound crept into her memory without having come there through her hearing? Better make sure.

She gazed once more at the hillside but could see nothing new, so she left her post and crawled up toward the ridge. If Po was still in his lookout she'd know it was a false alarm.

She was almost at the top when she heard the light click of a dislodged pebble. She froze. A moment later Po came crawling into view.

"Mana, do you not hear me call?" he whispered. "Why do you come? Why do you not hide?"

"Po, I think I hear," she told him. "I do not know. You saw a thing?"

"Men come," he said. "Three? Four? I do not know. They are careful. They move slow. They hide. Come. See."

He turned and crawled back to the ridge. More anxiously than ever Mana checked her own side of the promontory and then followed him. He was lying at the top of the ridge behind a boulder, peering down the far side. She wormed in beside him and very slowly raised her head to see past his. The long hillside seemed as empty as ever.

"See the big rock," he whispered. "It touches the reeds. See farther and up, a small cliff..."

Before he had finished, a brief flicker of movement caught her eye, well to her left, near the bottom of the slope.

And again.

This time, ready for it, she saw it more clearly, a dark someone or something darting between two boulders. Now the hillside was empty again. But again that quick, darting movement, across the same gap—another man, a second, and a third, and a fourth, each with his fighting stick held low, at least one with a skull at his waist.

There was something puzzling about their movements. Though they were obviously taking a lot of trouble to keep under cover, they weren't being clever about it. There, now, that one crouching behind that boulder. His head and right shoulder and arm were still in clear view.

"Po, they hide badly," she whispered.

"They came before," he suggested. "People were in those reeds. They found them. Now they say in their hearts, *People are there*. They hide from them. They do not hide from us."

Yes, that must be it. And now the four demon men were creeping down to the entrance to the path into the reedbeds. Just above it they stopped and searched the ground, once or twice pointing to some sign or mark one of them had spotted.

"What do they see?" said Po.

"I do not know..." Mana began, but then the answer

struck her. "Ah—Kern's body was there. We lifted it. We carried it away. They see this."

More cautiously than ever, the four men moved to the entrance to the path and followed each other in.

"They do not find us in the reeds," said Po. "Do they find their dead men? Mana, what do they do then?"

"I do not know," she said. "I think they look more. They come up the hill. They see the other side. Po, now I move the white stone. I say to the others, *Demon men are here*. Is this good?"

"Mana, it is good," he said. "I stay here. I watch."

So Mana turned back, but before she started down the western side of the hill she checked it carefully. Perhaps the demon men had sent a second party of scouts, and they were already there below her. But still nothing moved, so she crawled down to the lookout and laid the signal stone flat. Bodu, with Ojad on her hip, appeared briefly at the edge of the dead reeds, waved, and slipped out of sight again. Satisfied, Mana returned to the ridge and lay down beside Po.

Time passed. Every now and then Mana crawled back to check the western slope, saw nothing, and returned to Po. At long last the demon men emerged and stared around. What had they found? Mana wondered. Were the bodies of the two that she and Tun and Ridi had killed still floating in the water of the trap, or had they sunk out of sight? What did these men feel if they'd found them? Were they angry, as the Kin had been about Kern, full of feelings of revenge, more savage than ever? Or was it like when a jackal was killed, and the others of the pack just sniffed for a moment at the body and moved on? Both thoughts were dreadful, but the second one was worse.

The demon men weren't making any attempt to hide now. It didn't seem to occur to them that anyone might be watching from above. They hesitated a while, touching each other from time to time. The one with the skull at his waist began to point in various directions. Then they split up, one heading along the shoreline toward the tip of the promontory, two moving across it at different angles, and the fourth climbing up toward the two watchers. All four zigzagged to and fro as they went, keeping low but not taking any special trouble to hide, and covering as much ground as they could.

Mana and Po knew at once what they were doing. This was how a hunter moved when he'd lost the trail and was searching for some sign of his prey—a hoof-print, a rock disturbed from its bed, fur caught on a thorn, droppings.

"Soon he comes close," Po whispered. "Now we hide."

They left the ridge and crawled rapidly back down to the boulder with the slot beneath it. Mana was smaller than Po, so he wriggled in first and then she passed him the rock they would use to fill the final gap, checked that the other rocks were in easy reach, and worked her way in beside him. As soon as she was settled, they fitted the screening rocks into place, leaving themselves three narrow cracks of light. By twisting her neck until her cheekbone was hard against the rock beneath it, Mana could get her eye to the right-hand crack and see a narrow stretch of the hillside, and the reedbed beyond. Po was better off. He could reach both of the other cracks, and see a different bit of the slope through one, and through the other a long way out over the marsh, including the island where the Kin laired and had their fire.

So they lay in the dark and waited. While they had been watching unseen, up on the ridge, Mana had barely been afraid. Her heart had thundered at first, but more with excitement than terror. Then, as time passed, this had quieted to the sort of steady, intent awareness that she felt while fishing.

Now, though, the heavy pulse began again, and would not calm. Time passed, slowly, slowly, with nothing to measure it. It was not yet midday, so the sun was behind her, and every shadow on the patch of hillside that she could see was hidden by the rock that cast it, and she was unable to watch it shrink.

At last she felt Po reach for her hand and squeeze it. She moved to let him put his mouth close against her ear.

"One is below," he breathed. "He waits. He looks here. He raises his hand. I think another is near us....He moves....Now I do not see him."

Mana eased her head back to her spyhole. The wind was blowing steadily up the slope and whistling into the crack, so that if she tried to watch for any length of time her eye started to weep in the draft. She could see nothing new, but heard a soft call from somewhere down below. It was answered from very near by. A moment later Mana's narrow line of sight was briefly blocked by something moving across it, and on.

"One is here," she whispered. "He goes your way."

"I see him," Po breathed. "He goes down the hill, fast, fast. Now another comes....I think they find our sleep place."

Under the almost voiceless whisper, she could hear his excitement, and shared it, despite her fear.

For some time they saw nothing more. It was very frustrating. A little below their hiding place, but out of sight for both of them, was the area where the Kin had spent the last three nights and deliberately left the signs of their having done so. They could only guess whether the demon men had found them. But Bodu would still be watching from the reeds. She would have seen. Nar would now be racing along the path to bring the news to the island that the lair had been found....

Ah! There was a demon man!

Bent low, searching the ground, he crossed Mana's sight line and vanished.

"Smoke rises," whispered Po.

The man came back in the other direction, nearer. Before he moved out of sight Mana heard the same furtive call. The man looked up, turned, and stared across the marsh, shading his eyes. Mana held her breath. This was a crucial moment. Would they work it all out? Would they understand the signs and realize that their prey stayed far out in the marsh by day but slept the night here on the hillside? And then would they make up their minds that if they wanted to catch the Kin without having to fight their way along the maze of paths in the reedbed, full of traps and ambushes, they must come by night?

That was what the Kin were hoping for. Though Tinu's plan might work in other ways, a night attack would be far the best. Even then, the thought of all that could go wrong filled Mana with dread.

Now her man moved out of sight. Her eye was so sore from peering into the draft that she could scarcely see. She withdrew and rested it, blinking away the tears. She could hear nothing but the hiss of the wind and far bird-calls from the marsh.

She wondered what the demon men would be doing. From the way they had behaved when they had come out of the path in the eastern reedbed, it didn't look as if they had words. That was how the wordless people Mana knew, the Porcupines and the marshpeople, worked out what they were going to do. They touched each other and grunted and gestured until they had all agreed. Tor was Porcupine, and Noli was Tor's mate, but even Noli still didn't know how they did it.

"This one sees that one's mind, I think," she'd told Mana. "With Tor I do this little, little. For me it is hard. My mind is full of words."

It was strange to think of the savage killers on the hillside being in any way like the kind, gentle Tor. But there was no escape from it. They were people too. People, like Mana herself, and Po and Suth and Noli. And she, Mana, had killed one of them. Now she was helping to try to kill many more.

The horror of the thought shuddered through her. Po felt it, but didn't understand.

"Do not be afraid, Mana," he whispered. "This is good. Our trap works."

She sighed, knowing that it was no use explaining. He still wouldn't understand.

They lay in their hiding place until long past noon. Shadows appeared on the uphill side of the rocks and started to creep toward them. From time to time Mana peered through her crack, but saw no more of the demon men. Po could reach both of his cracks with either eye, and give the other one a rest. He saw the men several more times, lurking along the edge of the marsh. The entrance to the path was out of view, so he didn't know if they'd found it.

At last, Mana saw them again, climbing purposefully northward across the slope.

"I think they go," she whispered.

They waited some time more before pushing their screening rocks aside and crawling out, aching and stiff with long stillness. They climbed to the ridge and studied its farther side, but they could see no sign of the demon men, so they lifted the signal stone into place and crept down to the marsh.

Oldtale

Farj

Snake said in his heart, *Fat Pig's plan is good. I do it too. I go to my Kin. They are at Old Woman Creek. They do not eat snake. I hide in long grasses. I wait. I see Puy, their leader. I show myself to him. He sees me first. He hears my words.*

He went to Old Woman Creek. The men hunted zebra. The women foraged. Farj tended the fire. He was old. His limbs shook. He did not see well.

Snake said in his heart, *I do not speak with old Farj. He was a strong man. He was leader. That is gone. Now he is old, he shakes, he mutters, he sees few things. No, I wait for Puy.*

Farj prayed. This was his prayer:

Snake, you are strong, you are wise.
You guard your snakelings.
Hear me, Farj. I am old. Soon I die.
These are bad times, bad.
Rage is in the men's hearts.

My first son is dead, he is killed.
My second son seeks vengeance.
Soon he is killed also.
Let me die before this.
I, Farj, ask.

Snake heard him. He said in his heart, *This is my doing.* He spoke. He said, "Farj, my snakeling, I am sad for you, sad."

Farj did not see him well. He said, "Who speaks?"

Snake said, "I, Snake, speak. I am your First One."

Farj kneeled. He knocked his head on the ground. He clapped his hands together. He said, "Snake, First One, stop this fighting. Today the men hunt zebra. They dry meat, they put food in their gourds. Tomorrow they seek out the men of Fat Pig. They fight yet again. Speak to them, First One. Take the rage from their hearts."

Snake said, "Farj, I cannot do this. The men have sworn the War Oath. They must unswear it. From their hearts they must do it, not from my telling. My powers are gone. Black Antelope took them. Only one of my Kin hears my words. It is you."

Farj said, "First One, this is hard. Rage stops the men's ears. I speak, they do not hear. What do we do?"

Snake said, "Farj, I do not know."

He laid his ear to the ground. He heard a noise. It was like this:

See the mountain. Fire is inside it. Now it bursts out. Rocks fly through the air, they are red, they are hot. The mountain shakes, it roars. Far off men hear it. They listen. They say in their hearts, *This is not thunder. It is more.*

Such was the noise Snake heard.

He said, "We wait. One comes. He runs fast. He is heavy. It is Fat Pig."

Fat Pig came. Siku was on his back. They were tired. Black Antelope came with them. They did not see him.

Fat Pig spoke to Siku. Farj could not hear him. Siku said, "I am Siku. This is my First One. His powers are gone. Only I hear his words. We bring news. Soon the Kins go to Mambaga. They hunt the white-tail buck. You go by Beehive Waterhole. The men of my Kin sharpened their digging sticks. They set out. Now they lie in wait at the waterhole. Say to your Kin, *Do not go there*."

Farj said, "This is not good. The men have rage in their hearts. They say, *Ah, ah! Men of Fat Pig lie in wait for us. We go. We creep up on them from behind, softly, softly. We kill many.*"

Siku said, "Do you tell the women?"

Farj said, "Some are foolish. They speak to their men. Now, wait. I think."

He thought. He said, "We do thus and thus."

Black Antelope heard the words of Farj. He said in his heart, *This is good. Now I speak to the zebra. The men do not catch any.*

7

Three nights until big moon.

The attack could come on any of them, or on several more nights after. All of those would be light enough.

What if there were already demon men spying on the Kin's doings from farther along the ridge? This is what they would have seen. All day, the bare hillside and the occasional puff of smoke from the island, streaming away in the wind. Then, as the sun went down, two or three people coming cautiously out of the reedbed and anxiously scanning the hill for signs of danger. Apparently satisfied, they would turn and gesture, and other people—ten and ten and several more of them—would come out of the reeds, climb confidently up the hill and settle down for the night with a couple of sentries on watch.

Soon the moon would be up and the short dusk over. Now the whole western slope would be in deep shadow. So the watchers wouldn't see most of the sleepers rise from their places and move down the hill and sideways to a different place—a place screened from the north by a fold in the ground—and settle down again there.

But two people wouldn't go with them. One would stay at the old sleeping place, while the second—smaller than most of the others—climbed to the ridge and vanished.

This last person could only be Po or Shuja or Mana.

Everyone else but Tinu was too large to hide under the lookout boulder, and Tinu couldn't do it because she was unable to call the signal. The three chose pebbles from Suth's closed fist to decide in what order they would watch. Shuja watched the first night and saw nothing. Po watched the second, and it was the same. So Mana watched on the night of big moon.

She came out of the reeds with the others, climbed the hill, and pretended to settle down. When Tun whispered the word, all but Mana and Yova moved off to their real sleeping place. Yova stayed where she was and began her watch—at midnight Zara would climb the hill and take over, so that Yova could get some sleep. But Mana had to stay awake all night.

Bent low, she climbed the hill and into the moonlight. By now she knew the best route, crawling over the ridge itself along a shallow dip, down a gully beyond, and then left up the low spur that had the lookout at its top. By the time she was there the moonhawks were busy, calling from their nest site, skimming over the ridge, and hovering above the moonlit slope as they searched for prey.

Moonlight is deceptive. It seems almost as bright as day, but even the heaviest, darkest day is much brighter. Under the full moon Mana could see far into the distance along the rugged flank of the promontory, dark in the silvery light. She would have expected to be able to spot the demon men from a long way off as they came, no matter how carefully they hid as they crept toward her.

But as soon as the details of the plan had been worked out, even before the four demon men had come as scouts, Suth and Var had taken Mana, Po, and Shuja up to the ridge in the moonlight and told them to watch while he and Var walked away from them, making no effort to hide. In a terrifyingly short time they seemed to vanish. Only their moving shadows betrayed them, flickering over the gray rocks.

"The demon men come this way," Var had said, pointing north along the shoreline. "They know it."

"Var, you are right," Suth had said. "Few lead. They show the way. Many follow. They come by the shore. Then they climb the hill. They come here. It is above our lair. It is close. They wait. The moon goes up the sky. First it is on this side. The other side is dark. Then the moon is high. It shines on the other side. Then they attack."

Mana could only hope Suth and Var were right, but it did seem the obvious plan for the demon men—approaching by the route they knew, with a few scouts ahead, massing at the top of the ridge, and waiting for the moment when the moon rose just high enough to light the western slope, so that they could see their prey as they fell on them.

That was why Mana couldn't simply wait in the hiding place and give the warning from there. She wouldn't see the men in time for the Kin to reach the safety of the reeds. The attack would already have begun.

So now she crouched, as she had done so often by daylight, and watched the color of the hillside change slowly as the heavy shadows shrank toward the rocks that cast them. Above her the wind hissed and whistled between the boulders of the ridge, but down here she was in stillness. She didn't feel sleepy. She had spent the afternoon dozing on the island, and now in the certainty of danger, terror and excitement mingled into her bloodstream, pulsed through her at each beat of her heart, and kept her intensely awake and aware. Through the thick skin of her soles she could feel the grainy surface of rock, not just as surface but as individual grains that she could have counted if she chose. And she wasn't merely seeing the moonlit hillside. Her eyes seemed to feed on it, to suck it into her, until every mottling of the long slope seemed to be part of her, a tingle at a nerve end.

A flicker of movement. She tensed. Where? Ah, not among the rocks but above them. A star had vanished for an instant as something had passed it, a moonhawk swooping across the ridge to hunt in the brightness. She watched it briefly at its work, a shadow against the lit sky, speeding out along the wind, then swinging wide, slowing, hovering with fluttering wingtips while it peered with night-seeing eyes for anything that moved below it. She saw it plummet. Above the wind's hiss she heard the light thump of the strike and shrill squeal of the prey.

For an instant, hearing that squeal, Mana herself was the victim, cowering among these rocks, with the demon men poised to strike. Then she thought, No, this was different. The moonhawk did the thing it was made for, or it wouldn't be a moonhawk. But the demon men were people, just as she and the Kin were people. Each did the things they chose. The demon men chose to be demon men. But she, Mana, and the Kin chose to say, *No, we are not your victims.* Watching here on the hill was part of that choice.

She returned to her task, barely noticing the moonhawks any longer as they came and went. The night wore on. The moon climbed. Soon it would be high enough for its light to cross the ridge and reach the western slope. Soon, soon, surely, the attack must come, if it was coming tonight at all. Or had the demon men decided on a dawn raid? Or...

What was that? Down to her right?

No, it had been only the sudden plunge of a moon-hawk, followed by...

Not a squeal, not the thump of the strike, but a light squawk, and...

Why had it caught her attention? Why that strike, when she'd long stopped paying any attention to them?

She watched the bird circle up, but this time, instead of heading for the nest with its prey, or hovering again as it did when it missed a strike, it circled on, higher still, until she saw its spread wings actually cross the bright disk of the moon. No prey dangled from beak or talons.

Yes. That was it. She'd noticed the strike because something had been wrong with it. The hawk hadn't struck home. Even when it missed there was always the light thump of its impact with the ground. But not this time. And the squawk. Not from the victim, but from the hawk itself. A squawk of surprise. Of alarm.

What had it struck at? What quick, furtive movement? What shadow twitch, tricking it into danger? Surely it wouldn't strike at anything as big as a man. But what about a man crawling through a patch of shadow and allowing something, the tip of a fighting stick, a heel, a hand, to pass for a moment into moonlight?

Perhaps.

With her heart now slamming with panic, Mana stared. Where had the hawk dived? There.

So near?

She stared, but her night vision was dim from looking directly at the moon. Slowly it cleared, focussed on a single patch of the hillside...one low boulder...

Yes!

She had barely even a glimpse, but something had

moved, the tip of a larger something, a second man, per-haps, crawling behind the first. There was no time to wait for a third and make sure. They were so much near-er than she'd guessed.

Willing herself to move slowly she withdrew her head until she was completely under cover and hurried back the way she had come, until she reached the top of the western slope. It was still all in deep shadow, but the line where the moonlight met the darkness lay sharp along the dead reedbed, only a few tens of paces from the shore. The steady wind hissed over her.

While she waited to bring her heaving lungs under control she listened for the next call of the moonhawk. It didn't come. Of course—the bird had been alarmed. It was shifting its hunting ground. It wouldn't call again for a while.

"Wait," Suth had said. "Let the bird call. Call after it. Then you do not call together. We know it is the signal."

But she couldn't wait.

She cupped her hands, moistened her lips, drew a deep breath and called as loud as she could, because she was calling directly into the wind.

Yeek-yeek-yeek-yeek.

The call of the hunting moonhawk, made not three times but four. She and Po and Shuja had practiced it again and again down in the marshes, until even Var was satisfied that they had it true.

At once she took another breath and repeated the cry.

That was the signal, two calls, each of four shrieks. The closer the calls to each other, the closer the enemy.

They are here! They are close, close!

As the final shriek left her lips, she rose and hurried to the hiding place. The demon men were already terrifyingly near, but she didn't dare run. She had to feel for each footstep in the almost pitch-dark. Any noise she made would carry to them on the wind.

At last, with her heart thundering from the tension of stealth, she crouched down by the boulder and checked by feel that everything was where she needed it. But she didn't slide in under the rock at once. She could see too little from there. Instead she laid her body along its lower side, with her head projecting far enough beyond it to let her watch the jagged line of the ridge against the sky, paler and almost starless now as the rising moon drew nearer.

From below her, she could hear nothing but the movement of the wind, though by now the sentries would have awakened the sleepers on the hillside and they would all be moving stealthily through the darkness. A few of them would be climbing up to join Yova at the old lair—when the alarm came, the attackers must think that they had all been sleeping there, unsuspecting. The others would be creeping down to the reedbed. Most of these would immediately hurry along the hidden path to the island, but several of the men, with Tinu, would hide close by among the reeds. And Yova would be fully alert and tense, staring like Mana for the first glimpse of a movement on the skyline.

Again time passed, slow as the rising moon. Mana thought it would never reach the ridge, though the sky there now seemed almost as pale as dawn. Had she made a mistake and given a false alarm? Had the moonhawk's behavior tricked her into seeing a movement that wasn't there?

What was that?

Not a movement but a sound, a brief, faint scrape, barely reaching her through the wind. Wood on stone, perhaps? The trailing end of a fighting stick touching for an instant against a rock?

And now she saw a movement, a slow change in the jagged black skyline, as a head was stealthily raised to peer down the slope.

The man seemed to stay there for ever, watching what lay below him, though it was all still deep in shadow. Had he night vision, like a moonhawk? Would he see Mana herself, despite the darkness? He was so close above her.

She remembered something she had heard Suth say to Po when he was telling him how the hunter must think while he lay in wait for his prey: *I hide among grasses. I am grass. The buck does not see me.*

I am rock, she thought. *I lie long on this hill. I am still, still.*

At last the head withdrew, but Mana stayed where she was. It was too soon to go into her hiding place. She was to give the next signal when the enemy began to move down the hill, and from the hiding place she wouldn't be able to see that happen. Would they attack immediately from the ridge as the moon rose, or would they, more likely, try to use the darkness to creep nearer to their prey?

Ah, now they came. Mana saw several of them at once, slinking over the skyline and starting down the hill. Their fighting sticks were held low at their sides. All but one, and this man moved more awkwardly. Mana could see why. He had to hold his fighting stick two-handed because its point was weighted down by a round mass.

With a wrench in her stomach she guessed what it was. A human head. And she guessed whose.

She swallowed twice, mastering the shock of horror,

and silently squirmed herself back and then sideways, feetfirst, into the slot beneath the boulder. She didn't drag the smaller rocks into place, because the sound was certain to betray her, and she still needed to see out. So now she lay with only the top of her head outside the slot. With her right hand she reached out and felt for the base of the long reed that lay there, ready for the instant she needed it. At its other end was a small mound of rocks, which had been carefully balanced by Tinu at the top of a sloping slab.

Mana waited, scarcely breathing. She could no longer see the ridge, but she had a clear view down to the marsh and along the side of the promontory to her right. Below her the line of shadow had almost reached the shore. The slope was still in darkness, but the sky above was brilliant with stars and bright with the nearing moon. Before long, against that brightness, Mana saw the line of demon men creep past, spread out along the hill. The nearest one was not ten paces from her.

Just after he'd gone by she gave the reed a tug. The mound of rocks unbalanced and rattled noisily down the slab.

The demon man halted, turned, stared. Mana held her breath. Would he guess what had happened? Or would he think that he had somehow dislodged the rocks as he passed? Yova's yell of *Danger!* gave him no time to make up his mind.

Shrieks and screams rose from the lair, the handful of people there shouting at the top of their voices, sounding like three times their number, and continuing to make the hillside echo with their panic as they raced down the hill.

The line of demon men charged after them, their war cries doubling the din.

Mana raised her head to watch. The moonlight had reached the edge of the reeds. She could see the heads of people milling around by the path entrance, their bodies still in darkness—not many, but making it seem as if others had already passed through, and these were the last few struggling to get in, screaming with panic as they waited for their turn. The final one vanished into the reeds while the attackers were still charging down the hill.

This was the next critical moment. The leading demon men didn't hesitate but plunged in through the now obvious entrance. Would they all follow? Would anyone stay on guard? No. They all crowded through.

Now Mana crawled from the slot and, crouching in the shadow of the boulder, looked left and right along the hillside. No demon men watched there, either. Cautiously she raised her head into the moonlight and checked the ridge. That too was empty. She turned, cupped her hands around her mouth and screamed the moonhawk call at the top of her voice, twice and twice, *yeek-yeek…yeek-yeek.*

She waited and repeated the signal.

They are all gone in. None keeps watch.

Unsure if her voice would carry that far against the wind, she climbed onto the boulder, raised her arms over her head and waved them up and down, until at last she saw people slipping out from the reeds to the left and right of the entrance.

They waved to her to show that they had seen her, and all but one disappeared along the path where the demon men had gone to start dragging the reedstems off a series of new traps that had been prepared for this moment. The last one, Tinu, came racing up the hill with a bundle over her shoulder. Mana ran to meet her, took the bundle—dry reeds—and arranged them into a loose pile on a jutting rock. Tinu opened the fire log she was carrying and tipped the contents onto the pile.

There was no need for her to blow on the embers. The wind did that, setting them glowing at once. Mana fed them with loose wisps of leaves, which curled, crackled, and burst into flame. Within seconds, the whole pile was ablaze.

Out on the island and along the curving path to the left and right, watchers were waiting for the signal. They too had dry reeds piled and fire logs ready. Now it was Mana and Tinu's turn to stand with pounding hearts and stare and wait....

There! An orange spark!

And there! And there! Soon the reedbeds were alight at each place, and the sparks became brightnesses as the flames roared up, and fresh sparks shone and grew between them as the people out there raced along the path with twists of flaming reeds in their hands to start new fires, working all the time from the outer ends toward the safety of the island, in case an eddy of wind should cause the flames to swirl backward and set fire to the reeds behind them.

But the wind held steady and drove the flames before it, spreading them to the left and right, joining the separate blazes together, so that soon the watchers on the hillside saw two curving lines of flame stretching toward each other while the smoke, bright silver in the moonlight, streamed in front of them as they roared toward the shore, building a wall of flame to trap the demon men inside it and drive them back the way they had come.

By the time the two lines of fire joined into one, they were moving as fast as a man could run, certainly faster than a group of men who had been following what had seemed one simple path and then suddenly found themselves lost in a tangle of paths that led only into blind alleys in the middle of the reedbed—and then, when they realized their danger and turned to race back to the safety of the shore, found that path blocked by places where the footing suddenly gave way beneath them, leaving them floundering in thick engulfing mud, which they must either struggle through or fight their way around through the mass of reeds.

And all the time the smoke was streaming over them, and nearer and nearer they could hear the growl and crackle of the flames....

Tinu was jumping up and down in her excitement, clapping her hands, exulting not just in watching the destruction of these terrible enemies, but (perhaps even more) at the glory of seeing her huge trap working, just as she'd planned it. But Mana felt no such thrill. Mainly she felt a huge relief that things had gone so well, so luckily, and that the hideous danger they had been living with would soon be over.

But at the same time, with another part of her, she felt the horror of its needing to be done. That men, people, should die like this. Even at this distance, she could now hear the bellow of the flames, and mixed into them, faintly (or was that only her imagination?) screams. It had had to be done. But it was wrong, wrong.

She could no longer bear to watch or listen. She put her hands over her ears, turned away, and faced the slope. By now the moon was clear of the ridge, no longer silver, but browny orange behind the veil of smoke. Into the round of its disk flew a bird.

One of the moonhawks again, of course. But this time it didn't fly on. Full in the face of the moon it poised, hovering with wings spread wide. It seemed to be watching the scene below, just as Mana and Tinu had been doing. Perhaps it wasn't one of the nesting pair after all. Perhaps it was Moonhawk herself, come to see that all went well for her Kin.

A prayer formed itself in Mana's mind. Silently she breathed it between her lips.

> Moonhawk, I praise.
> Moonhawk, I thank.
> Let it be finished, Moonhawk.
> Soon, soon.

With a tilt of its wings, the bird swung away and was gone. Comforted, Mana turned back to the marsh.

The smoke was denser around them now as the flames marched closer. It streamed up the hill, hiding the shoreline. Shouts came from it suddenly, the voices of men in rage—the five Kin who had gone along the path to open the traps and had then returned to wait in ambush by the entrance, ready to strike down any survivors as they struggled through into the open. The path was only wide enough for one of the demon men at a time, as they were forced out by the closing flames, groping, blinded with smoke.

Tinu gave a cry, pointed, snatched up a rock, and raced to her right. Someone was running up the slope. Two others were chasing him, with digging sticks held ready to strike. Without thinking, Mana seized a rock and ran to cut the first man off, to delay him for just an instant.

All four shapes—Tinu, the two men of the Kin, and their quarry—disappeared in a swirl of smoke. It cleared, and she saw Tinu's throwing arm lash forward as the man rushed passed her. He staggered, missed his footing, half fell. Before he could recover, his pursuers were on him, beating him down with savage strokes.

Mana dropped her rock and turned away. Only later did she think how strange it was. If she had been the first to see the man escaping, she would have done exactly what Tinu had done, and rushed to try and delay him so that the men could catch and kill him. But seeing it happen had filled her with horror.

That was the last of the demon men to try to escape from the reeds.

When the tips of the curving line of flame met the shore they died away, and the curve itself closed inward until the two ends met and the fire died. Now there was nothing left for it to burn, but for a while ribbons of smoke continued to stream out of the charred mess beyond. Then they too dwindled and died and the night grew clear.

The group on shore, Mana, Tinu, and the five men, climbed halfway up the hill and waited, though they didn't expect the others to try to find their way out of the marsh until daylight when the embers of the great fire would be cool enough to walk on and they could see their way for sure.

Some kept watch, but Mana herself lay down and dropped into a wonderful, deep and dreamless sleep. She didn't wake until it was broad day. The others were already coming and going from the island or searching along the shore and around where the paths had been.

She could see the bodies of demon men lying by the entrance. Beyond them stretched a great black space, from which the wind picked up sudden flurries of ash flakes and floated them up the hillside.

Mana didn't go down to join her friends but waited until she saw the whole group gather together and come trooping purposefully up the hill. Tun led the way. In his hands he cradled a dark round thing. Kern's head. Mana guessed that the first thing they had done, as soon as it was light, was search for the leader's body. They would have found the head lying beside it.

Net had a wound in his side where a blind thrust from one of the demon men had caught him as they fought at the entrance. Moru had painful burns from a freak explosion of flame backward into the wind. Several of the others had lesser burns, and many had eyes still weeping from the smoke.

Chogi had already done what she could for these hurts. Now, before they fed or rested, Tun led them along the hill and up the headland to the mound where Kern was buried. They unpiled the rocks from Kern's body. Tun settled his head into place. They rebuilt the mound.

The women lined up to the east of it, with the rising sun behind them. The men sat facing them and beat out the rhythm with their hands, groaning in slow deep notes through closed lips. The women stamped to the time of the beat and set up the shrill interlacing wail that would loose Kern's spirit from the place where he had died and send it on its way to the Good Place on the Mountain, the Mountain above Odutu, where the First Ones lived.

Mana watched and listened, sensing all around her the others' feeling of rightness, of release at a dreadful act being at last undone and made well. She shared the feeling. She was glad for Kern, glad for herself and the Kin. But there were other spirits still bound to this hillside and the marsh below it. She could sense their presence also, the spirits of all the demon men who had been killed that night and earlier. She could almost feel them around her, almost hear them wailing faintly in the sweet morning air.

When the dance was over, they went quietly back

along the hillside, but as they crossed the spur that brought them in sight of the eastern marsh, the leaders halted. The rest climbed up to see why they had stopped. Down on the shoreline a single figure was dancing wildly. Ridi. Her savage chant of triumph reached them on the wind, as she exulted in the vengeance that had fallen on her enemies.

Mana watched, thinking, *No, I am not like that.* She realized that Noli was standing beside her.

"Noli," she whispered. "Help me. I have a trouble in my heart."

Noli seemed to be in some kind of dream. The death dance was First One stuff. Maybe she had gone part of the way with Kern on his journey. Now Mana saw the ordinary brightness come back into her eyes.

"Mana," she murmured. "What is this trouble?"

"Noli…it is these others…" said Mana. "They are demon men…They are dead…spirits…Where do they…How…?"

Noli understood the stammered question. She shook her head, smiling.

"Mana, I do not know," she said. "It is not our stuff. Soon we leave this place."

"Noli, it is my stuff," Mana insisted. "It is a trouble in my heart. What do I do?"

"Mana, I…" Noli began, shaking her head again.

She stopped, shuddered and clutched Mana by the shoulder. A dribble of froth appeared at the corner of her mouth. Mana put an arm around her, ready to stop her from falling, but it wasn't needed. The whisper of Moonhawk's voice was so soft that only Mana could hear it.

"Wait."

Noli sighed, shook herself and looked around. She frowned at Mana, puzzled.

"Moonhawk was here?" she asked. "She spoke?"

"Yes," said Mana. "It was for me."

The others were starting to move on. Noli nodded, shook herself again, and followed them. She didn't remember what had just happened, Mana realized, perhaps not even Mana asking her question.

That didn't matter. Mana knew what to do now. Wait.

Oldtale

The Pig Hunt

The men of Snake came back from their hunting. They were tired. They were hungry. They brought no meat.

They said, "Yesterday we saw many zebra. Today they are gone. We saw their tracks. All went together. We followed them far and far. We did not find them."

The women mocked the men. They said, "You are foolish hunters. The zebra are more clever. Tonight you eat plant stuff only. Your strength is gone."

The women laughed at the men. Their laughter was like this:

See, it is dusk. The starlings gather to their roost, the blue starlings. The sky is dark with their wings. They clamor with shrill voices. A lion roars. He is not heard. So loud are the voices of the starlings.

Such was the laughter of the women at the men of Snake. The men were ashamed.

It was dusk. Fat Pig went to the reedbeds of Old Woman Creek. He spoke to the pigs in their wallows.

He said, "The water goes. Soon these wallows are dry. Beehive Waterhole has good mud. Come now. It is night. The sun does not burn us. The moon is big. We see the way."

The pigs rose from their wallows. They went with Fat Pig.

Now a great snake lay in their way. By the moonlight they saw him. He reared himself up. He hissed. Fat Pig said, "Run! Run! It is a demon snake! It eats us all!"

Pigs are not wise. One does a thing, they all do it.

Fat Pig ran east, toward Yellowspring. The others followed. They came to Long Rock Ridge. Fat Pig stopped. They all stopped.

They said, "The snake is gone. Now we go to Beehive Waterhole."

They went. They walked on Long Rock Ridge. They made no tracks.

Fat Pig did not go with them. He went to Old Woman Creek. There he found Siku. She hid in long grasses. He said, "Climb on my back. I take you to Windy Cliff, to your own Kin."

It was morning. The Kin of Snake woke. They filled their gourds. They set out for Beehive Waterhole. Men led the way.

Soon they cried, "Ho! What is this? Here are tracks of pigs, many, many. See, they go this way, toward Beehive Waterhole. Pig are not zebra. They do not run far and far. Now we hunt these pig. We kill them, we eat them. Fat Pig are our enemies. We take their strength from them. Women, follow these tracks. We go fast."

Now they cried, "Ho! What is this? The pigs turn

aside. Something makes them afraid. See, they run fast. Soon they are tired. We catch them."

They followed the tracks. They came to Long Rock Ridge. The tracks were gone.

The men said, "Now they turn aside. Which way do they go? Beehive Waterhole is this way. Yellowspring is that way. It is nearer."

They went toward Yellowspring. The rock ended. They saw no tracks. They came back. The women were there.

The men said, "Now we go to Beehive Waterhole."

Farj said, "Yellowspring is nearer."

The women said, "Farj is right. Our small ones are tired. Our water gourds are empty. We go to Yellowspring. Men, do you come with us? We have plant food."

The men said in their hearts, *Plant food is better than no food.* They went to Yellowspring.

The men of Fat Pig lay in wait at Beehive Waterhole. No people came. Many pigs came. The men did not hunt them. Fat Pig do not eat pig.

8

Days of peace followed the battle. Tun still set lookouts from dawn to dusk and from dusk to the next dawn, but all the Kin knew in their hearts that they had dealt with the menace from the north. No great raid of demon men, people hunters, would come again. Nor were they likely to attack by twos and threes. If any were left where the others had come from, surely they were now afraid. And more than all that, Moonhawk was strong in this place. She would warn and protect her Kin.

Before anything else they took the bodies of the five demon men they had killed in the earlier skirmishes and carried them around into the burned area on the west. This cleared the eastern side of the promontory of anything that might attract demons, so that the Kin could settle back there to lair and fish and forage, and allow Tun's wound and Net's to finish healing and Moru to recover from her burns.

All the time Mana wasn't on lookout she spent at her fishing hole. She usually caught something, and one wonderful afternoon came back to the lair with four fish, all handsome and fat. But she was perfectly content to wait poised beside the hole, watch the minnows come and go, and catch nothing.

Fishing was good for her. She felt that she too had a wound to heal, a wound inside her, in her spirit. It had come to her with a blow from a digging stick. She had struck that blow with her own hand and arm as she had stood by the trap in the path through the reeds, with Tun sprawled beside her struggling to kick himself free from the demon man's grasp. She had hammered down on the demon man's head with Tun's digging stick, and at that third blow had felt the demon man's skull shatter. That was the moment she'd killed him. That was the wound in her spirit.

She had burns on her spirit too, not as deep as the wound, but sore. They were something like what had really happened to Moru. While Mana had been standing with Tinu on the hillside watching the smoke stream off the reedbed as the burning arc closed and closed, it was as if an eddy of wind had swirled over her, filled with the dark flame of the men's dying, and scorched her spirit as it passed.

So now she would wake in the middle of the night and everything would be still, apart from the faint hiss of the wind crossing the ridge above her. But Mana would be sure that just before she woke up she'd heard noises carried by that wind, the screaming of men trapped in the western reedbed as the wall of flame swept over them.

She didn't talk to anyone about this. As far as she could tell, the others, even Noli, felt nothing but triumph and relief at what they had done. Mana had those feelings too. She was happy that all of them except poor Kern were still alive, happy that the days were quiet and they could lair in safety around their fire on the hillside, happy in the beauty of the world, now that the wind had come to blow the haze off the marsh and let her see far into the sparkling distances. Happy to fish.

On the second day after the battle, two of the marshmen appeared from the reeds and climbed cautiously up to the camp. Shuja was on lookout, but didn't at once spot them as she was mainly watching for danger from the north. When she turned and saw them, she recognized them as friendly, so stood and hallooed down to the others, who were all foraging along the shore, or fishing, or searching the reeds for insect bait.

Mana came away from her hole and saw Tun and Var climbing the hill to greet the visitors. This wasn't child stuff, so she returned to her fishing. She heard what had happened when they were all sitting around the fire that evening.

"Two moons ago we came to this place," said Var. "One man was our guide. Then his two women were with him. They did not leave the reeds. Not the man, not the women. They were afraid."

"I saw this," said Net. "They were afraid."

There were murmurs of agreement. They could all remember.

"Now we fetched salt—I, Var, and Net and Kern and Yova," Var continued. "Again we saw this man. We met him in the reeds, on a path. He sees us. He is afraid. He turns away. I call, *We meet well.* He runs. I call again. He stops. He comes back, slow, slow. He touches me. He smiles. He is happy. Now he is not afraid. He calls to his women. They come, afraid, afraid. They touch me. They are happy. I say in my heart, *These people think Var is dead. He is a spirit.* They touch. I am warm. I am not dead. They are happy."

"Var, you are right." said Yova. "I saw this."

"I say this," said Tun. "The marshpeople fear the demon men. They say in their hearts, *These strangers are fools. They go to the places of the demon men. The demon men kill them.* They hear fighting in the night. They see great burning. Then they see our fire on the hill. It is still there. They ask, *Do the strangers live?* They come. We take them to the dry reeds. We show them the bodies of demon men. They are happy. They are like Ridi. They give great praise. Soon more marshpeople come. They see too."

They talked it over for a while and agreed that Tun was probably right, but they weren't ready for the way it happened. This time Mana was on lookout. She heard a strange noise rising from the marsh behind her, and coming nearer and nearer. After a little while she realized that she'd heard it before, when the procession of marshmen had carried to their central island the head of the monster crocodile that the Kin had trapped and killed.

It was the sound the marshpeople made by banging together two of the reed tubes they carried at their belts. But this time it was different. When Mana had heard it before it had been a wild, dancing rhythm, mixed with shouts of triumph. Now it was slow and solemn and monotonous, with no intermingling of human voices. Mana recognized at once that it must be a death sound.

All the Kin heard the sound too, and left whatever they'd been doing to watch the procession. Tens and tens and tens of marshpeople, men, women, and children, came out of the reeds and climbed the hill toward the camp. Then there was the usual exchange of gifts. Even from the lookout point up on the hill Mana could see that the marshpeople had brought far more than the Kin could possibly give them in exchange.

After that the procession moved out of her sight, around to the western side of the promontory, but the marshpeople's sad music was carried to her on the wind all morning. As soon as Nar came up to take over as lookout she climbed to the ridge and looked down.

Far below her on the scorched mudbank, women and children were moving to and fro, searching the ground, while the men stayed at the shoreline, steadily banging their tubes together. Every now and then one of the searchers would stoop, pick something up, and carry it to the shore to add to a pile. Though she couldn't see for sure at that distance, Mana realized at once that they were collecting the skulls that the demon men had carried at their belts.

And she knew too—the noise from the sound sticks told her—that what they were doing wasn't demon stuff. It was the opposite. They were taking the skulls not as trophies, like the great crocodile head, but so that they could do something good with them. Some of these skulls must have belonged to marshpeople, but they didn't know which, so they were taking them all. They would feel about them much as the Kin had felt about Kern, so they'd want to do something like the Kin had done when they had returned Kern's head to his body, where it belonged, and only then had done the death dance for him.

When they finished they grunted their farewells and filed off into the reeds, with the sad music of the sound-sticks growing fainter and fainter as they moved away.

They had left a great pile of gifts, mostly fish, but also fishing sticks and crocodile teeth and braided belts and belt tubes. Some of the tubes had in them the colored paste the marshmen used to paint their faces, so the children had a great time covering each other with red and yellow and purple blotches and streaks. That night the Kin feasted until everybody's stomach was crammed.

The next day Var and Suth set out on a scouting expedition to the north. Three anxious days later they returned, tired but well, to say that they had gone all the way up the promontory along the same endless barren slope, and then climbed a range of hills that were almost mountains, almost barren too, with no sign of Good Places for the Kin to live in. They'd nearly run out of food and were getting desperate by the time they reached the top, but had gone on farther and looked down into a huge valley, full of promise, just the sort of area they'd been hoping for. They'd explored a little, and seen few signs of people, but they'd found plenty to eat.

When they had finished their report Tun praised them with strong words. Then he said, "This is good. Tomorrow we go. We find new Places. Be ready."

The next morning, as soon as it was light, Mana went to her fishing hole for the last time and dribbled scraps of bait into it, then watched the little fishes come to gobble them up. To her delight a beautiful large fish appeared, silver with a yellow stripe along its flanks. It was one of the best sort, with pinkish flesh, juicy and firm, but she didn't try to catch it. Instead she gave it extra bait, and blessed it and the little ones and the water they swam in, and left feeling both sad and happy.

The Kin traveled steadily up the promontory all morning, picking their way along the awkward slope with two men scouting ahead for danger. While they were resting Mana noticed Suth stop what he was saying to the other men and point across the marsh. She looked and at once saw what he'd seen. A long way out a line of tiny figures was wading thigh deep across a patch of open water.

"Ho! The marshpeople come too!" said Zara. "Now they are not afraid."

Net jumped to his feet, cupped his hands to his mouth, and hallooed and waved. After a pause Mana saw the marshpeople stop and turn. Everyone stood up and waved. The marshpeople waved back and moved on, while the Kin sat down, feeling cheered that they were not alone in their adventure.

"They use an old path," said Var. "They know it."

"Var, you are right," said Chogi. "I say this. All the marsh was their place. They fished here. They came to the dry land. They were not afraid. Then demon men came. They killed men, they took women. The marsh-people were afraid. They went away to the marsh. Now we kill the demon men. They are not afraid. They come back."

"Chogi, you are right," said Net, and they all agreed it seemed like that.

That evening they camped early, a little way up from the base of the promontory, where the shoreline swept away eastward at the foot of a great range of hills. As Var and Suth had warned them, these hills gave no promise of food, so they needed time to fish and forage among the shore plants.

As usual when they camped anywhere new, they made their fire in a hollow, so that it couldn't be seen from any distance. Tun set lookouts, and they scattered to their various tasks. There were rich pickings. No one seemed to have foraged here for many moons. Mana found a fong beetle's burrow with the guardian beetle lurking inside the entrance. It had a viciously poi-sonous bite, but she lured it into the open by tickling it with a grass stem and then squashed it with the rock she had ready in her other hand. Now it was safe to dig into the burrow and scoop the juicy brown bugs into her gourd.

Just as she finished she heard a brief whistling hiss from the reeds beside her. She looked and saw a bright-painted face peering at her between the reedstems. She held up her hand and called a soft greeting, and the marshman came cautiously out. She didn't recognize the pattern on his face, but he seemed to know who she was. He returned her greeting but looked past her, studying the hillside, and made a questioning sound, like a light bark but with his lips closed. Though it wasn't the grunt the Porcupines would have used, it was obvious what he was asking her.

Is it safe? Have you seen any demon men?

Mana smiled and grunted reassuringly and said, "Come, I take you to Tun." But when she started to lead the way he barked at her to wait and called to somebody among the reeds. Several more marshpeople came creeping out, men and women, all obviously very scared and anxious. One of the women offered Mana a couple of fishes as a gift, but wrinkled her nose in disgust when Mana tried to give her a few fong grubs in exchange.

Tun arrived and led them up to the camp. More marshpeople appeared, and by dusk ten and five more of them were sitting around the fire with the Kin and toasting their fish on its embers.

The marshpeople went back down the hill to sleep among the reeds—they didn't seem to mind about the sickness—but the next morning Mana was hardly awake when she heard a soft call from one of the lookouts. Five marshmen were climbing the hill. There were no women with them, and this time their whole bodies, not just their faces, were painted in brilliant colors.

"They come to fight," said Suth. "I remember this. They came to take the crocodile head. It was ours. They said in their hearts, *These people do not give us the head. We must fight them.* But Tun gave it to them. We did not fight. Then they were painted like this."

"Suth, do they fight us?" said Po.

"No. This is my thought. They fight the demon men. We did not kill them all. Some stayed in their own place."

The marshmen had brought no gifts this time. They exchanged greetings and then just stood around, obviously waiting for the Kin to move on. As soon as Tun gave the signal to leave, three marshmen ran on ahead as scouts, while the other two fell in beside Tun. They clearly knew where they were going, so he let them lead the group at a slant across the hill until they reached a ridge, which they then followed toward the summit.

It was a long and tiring climb. At last Mana saw that the scouts were beginning to move more cautiously, and when they finally disappeared over the skyline, the two marshmen walking with Tun made everyone else stop and wait until the scouts returned and signaled that it was safe to go on.

They climbed to a pass with hills rising on either side, and wound for a while along it, until the ground began to drop away at their feet and they could look north.

Mana heard a sigh from many mouths, and then a whisper from her left. She didn't know who'd spoken, but it was her own thought. It was everyone's thought.

"These are Good Places. Good. Good."

Oldtale
The Mambaga Crossing

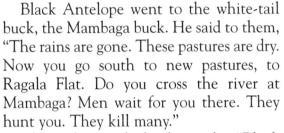

Black Antelope went to the white-tail buck, the Mambaga buck. He said to them, "The rains are gone. These pastures are dry. Now you go south to new pastures, to Ragala Flat. Do you cross the river at Mambaga? Men wait for you there. They hunt you. They kill many."

The white-tail buck said, "Black Antelope, we know the Mambaga crossing. We do not know another."

He said, "Now I show you another way. Come."

He led them east and then south, to Smoke Gorge. In those days the river was full of water. At Smoke Gorge it fell over a cliff.

The white-tail buck said, "Black Antelope, we cannot cross here. The gorge is too wide. It is too deep. The water smokes. It roars. We are afraid."

Black Antelope struck the northern cliff

with his hoof. It fell into the gorge. He leapt the gorge. He struck the southern cliff with his hoof. That too fell. The rocks lay across the gorge. The water was stopped.

Still the white-tail buck were afraid. Black Antelope leapt the gorge again. He said, "Come quick. The water rises. Soon the rocks are pushed away."

He led the white-tail buck across the rockfall. Their crossing was like this:

See, it is dawn. The ants leave their nest. All day they come, they go. They forage here, there. Now it is dusk. They gather to their nest. Who can count them? The ground is black with them. Through a narrow place they go into the nest. They are all gone.

Such was the crossing of the white-tail buck. The water rose beside them. The last buck crossed. The water burst through. It pushed the rockfall away.

The white-tail buck went south to Ragala Flat. There the grass was fresh, it was green. They were happy.

All the Kins gathered at Mambaga. They waited for the white-tail buck. None came to the crossing.

The men spoke to each other. They said, "Why do the buck not come? This is strange."

Farj had a daughter, Rimi. Her mate was Nos. He was Crocodile. Farj went to him. He said, "Nos, mate of my daughter, hear me, Farj. I am old. I have seen many things. This I have not seen. Always the white-tail buck come to Mambaga. At this season they come. Now they do not come. Why is this? I, Farj, say this. I am Snake. Our men swore the War Oath. Anger is in their hearts. The men of Fat Pig swore the War Oath. Anger is in their hearts also. The white-tail buck smell this anger. They are afraid. They do not come."

Nos said, "Farj, you are right. I speak to the other Kins. I tell them your words."

All the men listened. They said, "Nos is right. Farj is right."

They went to the men of Snake and of Fat Pig. They said, "Stop this war, this foolishness."

The men of Snake and of Fat Pig answered, "We cannot stop it. We have sworn the War Oath."

The men of the Kins said, "Our young men do not come to you. They do not say, *We choose your daughters for mates.* Your young men come to us. We say to them, *Our daughters do not choose you for mates.* First you end this war."

The men of Snake answered, "Let Fat Pig end the war first. Let them unswear the War Oath. Let them give us Mott. We kill him. Then we unswear the War Oath. We give them Ziul."

The men of Fat Pig answered in the same way. Both said, "We do not do it first. We do not lose face."

The women said, "You are fools." They did not laugh.

Farj and Siku listened to this talk. They told it to Snake and to Fat Pig.

Fat Pig and Snake said, "The men are ripe berries. They are ready. Farj, you are old, you are wise. What do we do now?"

Farj thought. He said, "Now we do thus and thus."

9

It was as if they had come into a different world. Behind them lay the long dry hillside and the pass— rocks, gravel, clumps of harsh grass, thorny stunted bushes scattered here and there, all brown and burned and weary, even after the rains. A world that was almost dead.

But here, so short a distance to the north, was a world of life, green slopes where deer could browse, wide-branched trees with cool shade beneath them, birds answering and calling, vines, bushes, smells of sap and pollen, the hum of honeybees, movement of creatures in the mottled shadows—good earth, good air, good foraging, good hunting—one immense Good Place spread out below them.

A thought came to Mana. She couldn't quite put it into words. Suth was standing beside her. "Suth," she whispered. "The demon men...They had this...all this...Why?"

Why had they left this wonderful valley to hunt and kill, not animals for food, but men, to cut their heads off and carry them away as...? As what? What did they want them for? Could their First One really be a demon? Did it tell them this was what they must do to please it? That was too ghastly to imagine.

Suth seemed to understand her stammerings. He frowned, shaking his head.

"Mana, I do not know," he said. "It is strange, strange."

Tun, of course, set lookouts, and the rest of the Kin started to forage. This wasn't what the marshmen wanted. They waited for a while, and then tried to persuade Tun to move on. When they realized he wasn't going to, they were unhappy, but hung around a little longer, grunting and gesturing and touching each other, and then went off down the hill, moving warily and holding their fishing sticks ready for fighting.

The Kin worked cheerfully, finding all they wanted, nuts and fruit and roots, grubs and birds' eggs. It had been well after midday when they'd started, and they hadn't had their usual rest, but the air was cooler at this height, and the excitement and pleasure of exploring this new home buoyed them up. Late in the afternoon Mana heard the shouts of hunters, and a little later Net and Nar appeared, triumphantly carrying the body of a large anteater they had surprised and killed.

By then they'd harvested more than enough, so Tun led them back up to the pass and found a good hollow for their lair. The night would be cold up here, but it was safer to sleep in the open, with lookouts on watch, than it would have been lower down, with so much cover for any enemy or wild beast to use to creep up on them.

In the dusk the five marshmen returned. With them came a woman who looked just like one of the marshwomen. She carried a girl baby.

The marshmen were in high spirits. They'd arrived making gestures of triumph, punching the air with their fists. Two of them carried skulls, which they laid carefully down a little way from the fire. Then they proudly showed their fishing sticks to Tun and the other men.

"What is this?" whispered Moru, watching from the women's side of the fire.

"I smell blood," said Noli. "I think they kill people."

Mana too had smelled the unmistakable odor, but hadn't guessed what creature it might belong to.

"Who is this woman?" said Shuja. "Do the marsh-men kill her mate? Do they take her? She is not sad."

The woman had come to sit with them opposite the men, and as Shuja had said looked dazed but not unhappy. She ate without seeming to notice what she was doing and kept her eyes fixed on one of the marsh-men on the other side of the fire.

"I say this," said Chogi decisively. "These people were not always marshmen. The marshmen were their friends. But these lived here. These Places were theirs. Then demon men came. They killed men, they took women. These men fled into the marsh. The marshmen said, *Be with us. Learn our ways.* They did this. Now we kill many demon men. These men say in their hearts, *We go back to our own Places. We find our women. We see a demon man. We kill him.*"

"Chogi, you are right," said Yova.

"Why do they bring skulls?" asked Bodu.

"A demon man kills their friends," suggested Moru. "He takes their heads. Now these men kill him. They take the heads back. This is good."

They discussed the idea for a while, but Mana was still thinking about the demon men. She could under-stand what the marshmen seemed to have done. That was revenge. It was dreadful, but it was people stuff. What the demon men did was different.

Did that mean they weren't people, after all? No, she knew in her heart they were. It was being people that was the worst thing about them. If they'd been just peo-ple-shaped animals, they'd still have been terrifying, but it would have been a different sort of terror. The demon men were men, like good, strong Tun and Suth, like excitable Net, like gentle Tor—that was what made the difference. And that was why Mana carried a wound in her spirit, because she had killed one of them.

One day, perhaps, she would understand. Moonhawk had told her to wait. So Moonhawk had known that Mana's wound was a real wound. She'd known that the demon men were people, or she wouldn't have said that.

The Kin slept by the fire, huddled in piles for warmth. The marshmen, the woman they'd found, and her baby made another pile of their own. In the morning they exchanged good-byes, and the marshmen headed back to the marsh, while the Kin went down into the valley to explore farther.

This time they moved faster, with scouts in advance, stopping to forage only if they came to an especially rich area. They found a small stream, splashing from boulder to boulder, and drank its clean, fresh water, but didn't trouble to fill their gourds.

They were following the stream, spread out in a loose line on either side of it, when Mana saw Tor, who was scouting in front of her, crouch and peer ahead, at the same time making a quick downward gesture with his left hand. Instantly she ducked into the cover of the nearest bush. When she looked left and right, the rest of the Kin seemed to have vanished, except for Tinu, who was crouching on the other side of the same bush.

They waited while Tor and Net crept out of sight.

Before long Tor returned and waved them on, but then made the same downward gesture as before—*Come. Keep low.* Everyone rose from their hiding places and stole forward.

They reached the rim of a hollow, halted, and looked down. The bank was short but steep. Below her, Mana saw what she instantly recognized as someone's regular lair. There was a dead fire with a large mound of ashes heaped up from steady burning over many days, a stack of branches for fuel, a trampled patch of earth, a flat boulder with drifts of seedhusks around it, and so on. The only unfamiliar thing was a pair of posts driven into the ground on either side of the trail that led on down the hill.

A body lay facedown beside the fire. Its skin was very dark gray, faintly tinged with purple, and streaked with blood from several small, deep wounds.

Mana heard a mutter beside her. Bodu.

"The marshmen killed him. They used fishing sticks."

Yes, a speared fish would have had a hole like that in its side. Chogi had been right in her guess last night. The body wasn't that of a demon man, though. It was too small. He'd been a boy—about Mana's own age, she guessed. A demon boy.

With a heavy sigh she bowed her head and turned away. Why? And why in this beautiful place, this lair by the tumbling stream…?

She couldn't bear to stay there, but crept off, tears for the dead boy beginning to stream down her face. She wept for him as she had wept for Kern. For the moment it was the same death.

She stole quietly on through the haze of tears, letting her feet choose the path. She knew that this was wrong of her, bad, allowing herself to lose sight of the others in this unfamiliar place with its unknown dangers. But she needed to be alone, to endure her grief without anybody speaking to her, trying to comfort her. She wasn't ready for that.

She stopped because she could go no farther, and wiped her tears away with the back of her hand, and looked around. She had reached a small clearing beside a fallen tree. She could still hear the whisper of the stream behind her. She wasn't yet ready to turn back. She felt unraveled, as if the sudden upwelling of pure grief had loosened the strands of her inward self—much as the braids of grass stems that she used to carry her gourd sometimes came untwisted—and she needed a little time to weave them firm again.

She was standing there, sighing and shaking her head, when someone shouted behind her. She jumped with alarm, then realized it was only Suth calling for her. As she was turning to answer, something hissed low down beside her. Again she jumped, then backed away, staring. A thin, dark arm slid out from under the fallen tree and beckoned to her. She kneeled and peered into the dark space beneath the trunk. Two wide eyes glistened. She could barely make out the shape of the face around them. A girl? A woman?

Suth called again, nearer. The arm beckoned impatiently. Mana held up her hand, palm forward—*Peace*—and answered over her shoulder, "Suth, I am here."

She rose and went to meet him. "Wait, Suth," she said softly. "One hides. She is afraid. She says in her heart, *These men kill me.*"

"I fetch Noli," he said, and ran off. Mana returned to squat by the fallen tree where the woman could see her, and smiled and made calming noises in her throat until Noli arrived with Amola. She crouched and looked in under the tree trunk and made the usual hum of greeting. When the girl—or woman—didn't move, Noli settled down cross-legged and put Amola to her breast, where she immediately began to suck happily.

Mana saw the round eyes widen. Slowly and cautiously, their owner crawled into the open. She was a strange little woman, obviously an adult but not as tall as Mana when she stood up. Her skin was darker than

Mana's, almost black. She had wide hips, and her face was wrinkled, like a newborn baby's, but otherwise she didn't look very old. Her eyes kept darting from side to side. She was as shy as a startled deer.

Noli rose, smiling, and took her hand.

"Come," she said, and led the way back toward the lair. The moment the woman saw Suth she gave a gasp of alarm, snatched her hand from Noli's, and backed away. Suth gave the *Peace* gesture and hummed a greeting. Hesitantly, the little woman edged back to Noli and let her lead her on.

Before they reached the lair, Suth called out to the others, "Hear me. We bring a stranger woman. She is afraid, afraid."

A few of the Kin climbed up the bank to meet her, and once again she stopped and backed away. Then, suddenly, she seemed to make up her mind that these newcomers meant her no harm, but she ignored their greetings and hurried on past them and out of Mana's sight down to the lair. Mana couldn't bear to look at the dead boy again, so when they moved on she asked Shuja what had happened.

"She turned the boy over," said Shuja. "She looked at him. My thought was, *He is her son.* But she did not grieve. She went to the fire. She took ash. She put it on his face. She stood a little. She turned away. It was finished."

"This is strange," said Bodu. "Is she a demon woman? I say *No.*"

They talked about it as they moved on, working generally eastward along the slope and not going farther down into the valley, so that they wouldn't have far to climb to the open ground when they wanted to lair that night.

"I say this," said Chogi at last. "Her skin is black.

The skin of the demon men is dark, like ours. The boy's skin is darker. A demon man took this woman. He was the father. The boy is her son. She does not want him. But he is her son."

"This is sad, sad," said Bodu.

The little woman didn't seem to think so. She had tagged along with them, seeming much more confident now, behaving as if she had always been one of their group, and foraging unconcernedly with them whenever they paused to do that. She seemed to have forgotten all about the dead boy.

But around midday, when they were starting to look for somewhere pleasant to rest and eat, she made one of her strange sounds and smiled and raised her hand in what was obviously a good-bye gesture, and then ran off down the hill. A little later they heard her call. Two more distant calls answered, one after the other.

"She finds friends," said Bodu. "Do we go see?"

Before anyone could answer, Mana saw Ridi fall on her knees in front of Tun, making the moaning whine that meant she was begging a favor. She pointed the way the little woman had gone.

"These are women's voices," said Tun. "We find them. We give gifts. They are friends. Is this good?"

They set off, with Ridi hurrying ahead, every now and then turning to wave to them to follow faster. After a bit she stopped and called. An answering cry came from below. Ridi broke into a run and disappeared.

They followed and met her farther down the hill, leading another woman back toward them. This one had a child on her hip, a girl a little younger than Tan. The mother looked very like Ridi, or one of the marsh-women, but the child's skin was darker, with a grayish tinge. The mother and Ridi were obviously old friends, laughing and crying with the happiness of their meeting.

They greeted Tun and then led the way to another lair, like the first but larger and with its fire still burning. There were two more women here, the one Mana had found that morning, and another who might have been her sister, with the same wrinkled face, black skin, and wide hips. She had a small baby, also very black. There was an older girl, black too, and a little boy with much paler skin. Ridi's friend seemed to be the boy's mother.

The other difference about this lair was that there were four posts at its entrance. At the top of each of them was a human skull.

This was a sight they were going to see several times over the next few days—a long-used lair with a fire burning at its center, women and children preparing food or foraging somewhere nearby, and two or more poles, topped by their ghastly trophies.

The women were mostly like the marshpeople, slight and pale skinned; some were like the strange little woman Mana had found by the lair with the dead boy; but a few were tall and thin with the same purple tinge to their dark gray skin as the demon men. The children were mixtures of these shapes and colors, but again a few of them had the true demon-people look.

When the Kin chanced on one of these lairs, the little women at once scuttled off and hid, and the pale-skinned ones started to do the same until Ridi called to them, when they came hesitantly back. But if there was a demon woman she would rise and face them proudly, with her demon child at her side. Neither of them looked as if they knew what it was like to be afraid.

The first time this happened Mana just stared at the two of them, but when the Kin moved on she found herself wishing she'd done more—greeted them, smiled, spoken—anything to show them, and show herself, that she and they were the same, that they were all people. So the next time, a couple of days later, she walked up to a demon woman and greeted her with the raised hand and the hum that the marshpeople used.

The demon woman glanced at her and away. The boy—a small one, just old enough to run without falling down all the time—stared back at Mana with dark, unfriendly eyes. She smiled and reached out a hand to touch him.

Instantly the mother hissed like a snake and snatched her son out of reach. Mana backed off, still trying to smile, but the mother stared fixedly away. When Mana turned, she saw several of the Kin watching her. Chogi shook her head, frowning. Mana felt very depressed when they moved on. She didn't try to make friends with a demon woman again.

All this was bad enough, but then there came a yet more dreadful change. By this time, the Kin had ventured farther down into the valley and were working their way back west, exploring as they went. Now when they chanced on a camp it was like the first one they'd found. The skulls had been taken from the poles. The fire was dead or dying, and sometimes there was a body or bodies lying beside the cold embers, demon women and dark-skinned children. Any other women and children were gone. Though Ridi called and called, no one answered.

The Kin stared at these scenes with a horror like Mana's. For a man to kill a woman or a child was a shame beyond shame. His own Kin were outcast until they hunted him down. His own brother, if he had one, would strike the blow. There would be no death dance. Instead his body would be carried to one of the demon places and left there for the demons to eat his spirit. His name would be deliberately forgotten. In the long history of the Kins only three such names were remembered, and only as a kind of warning. Da. Mott. Ziul.

The Kin saw no demon men at all, dead or alive, and to Mana's relief they met none of the marshmen who had done these killings. They had always seemed to be friends to the Kin, despite their strange ways, but now she didn't know how she could have faced them.

"We do not stay here," said Tun. "This place is full of spirits. They are demon spirits. No one does the death dance for them."

So he led them rapidly on westward and then north until they reached a much less fertile area where there seemed to be no old lairs at all. This was like the country they had been used to, more open, with its Good Places scattered far apart and almost barren stretches between them—rock, sand, gravel, coarse sunbaked grass, and harsh thorny bushes.

Here the Kin all found that they were more comfortable in their own spirits. It was as if life on those north-facing slopes had been too easy, too rich, too generous. They were talking about this by the fire one evening when a strange idea came to Mana. She thought about it a little and then touched Noli's arm.

Noli looked at her and raised her eyebrows inquiringly.

"I have a thought, Noli," Mana whispered. "The demon men. They trouble me. Why do they do these things? I say this. Those other Places—they are too good. The women do everything. They forage, they set traps. They find food, plenty, plenty. What do the men do? They hunt, they catch deer, two, three—there are many deer, many. They cannot eat all these deer. They say in their hearts, *I have nothing to do—I hunt people.* Is this man stuff, Noli? Does Tun do this? Does Suth?"

Noli took the question seriously, and thought about it, frowning.

"Mana, I do not know," she said. "Not all men do this. I know Tun does not do it. I know Suth does not do it. But men must do something. A man says in his heart, *Let people see me. Let them say, 'This is a man.'*"

Yes, Mana thought, that was it. Men needed to stand by the fire and boast about what they'd done. In the Kin they usually boasted about hunting, because hunting was difficult, and a successful hunt was something to boast about. But suppose hunting had been easy, what else was there? There was fighting, man against man. If a man killed another man, he was the better man. And to back up his boast, he might take the dead man's head.

Mana fell asleep that night feeling very depressed and still thinking about it.

Was it so? Did it have to be so?

Oldtale

The Game of Pebbles

The Kins left Mambaga. They said, "Let there be no fighting. Let Fat Pig go west, by Beehive Waterhole. Let Snake go east, by Yellowspring."

The Kin of Fat Pig journeyed a morning. A pig stood in their way. The pig was fat.

They said, "This is strange. This pig does not run from people. Why is this?"

Siku said, "I, Siku, show you."

She went forward. She was small. The pig lay down. Siku climbed on its back. The pig stood up. Siku said, "Come."

The pig went toward Yellowspring.

They said, "Do we follow? The Kins said, *Go by Beehive Waterhole.* We go to Yellowspring, they are angry. But see, this pig does not run from us. A child, a girl child, climbs on its back. She speaks thus to the elders. She is not afraid. Is this First One stuff? We follow this pig. We see."

They went toward Yellowspring. By the west trail they went.

The Kin of Snake journeyed to Yellowspring by the north trail. They came near the place. A snake lay in their path, a great tree serpent, green and black.

They said, "This is strange. Here are no trees. Here is this tree serpent. It does not hide from people. What is this?"

Farj said, "I, Farj, show you."

He went forward. The tree serpent raised itself. It coiled around him. Its head lay on his shoulder. It did not squeeze him.

He said, "Wait."

His Kin looked at him. They said, "This is old Farj. He shakes. He mutters. But see, the snake coils around him. It does not squeeze him. Is this First One stuff? We wait."

It was evening. The sun was low. The Kin of Fat Pig came near to Yellowspring. The pig stopped. Siku climbed from its back. The pig ran. It was gone. The people were thirsty. Their gourds were empty. They went to the spring. They came to it by the west trail.

So with the Kin of Snake. The tree serpent uncoiled itself from old Farj. It was gone. The people were thirsty, their gourds were empty. They went to the spring. They came to it by the north trail.

At Yellowspring the two Kins met. The men saw their enemies. They said, "Now we fight. Here this war began. Here we end it."

The women seized their arms. They said, "This end is foolish, foolish. Do not fight."

The men said, "People were killed, blood fell from wounds, fierce blows were struck. All this must be paid for. A death for a death, a wound for a wound, a blow for a blow."

Farj stood before his Kin. Black Antelope went

behind him. No one saw him. He breathed upon Farj.

Farj cried in a strong voice, the voice of a leader, "This is good. I, Farj, make the count for you. I count our deaths, our wounds, our blows. We are Snake. A snake coiled itself about me. It laid its head on my shoulder. This was a sign to you. I am chosen."

The men said in their hearts, *Fat Pig killed his son. Farj does not forget this. He seeks vengeance.*

The women said in their hearts, *One son lives still. Farj does not want his death. He seeks peace.*

Both said aloud, "We saw this sign. Let Farj make the count for us."

Siku stood before her Kin. Black Antelope went behind her. No one saw him. He breathed upon Siku.

Siku cried in a clear voice, the voice of a senior woman, "This is good. I, Siku, make the count for you. I count our deaths, our wounds, our blows. We are Fat Pig. A pig stood in our way. It lay down. I climbed on its back. It led you to Yellowspring. This was a sign to you. I am chosen."

The men said in their hearts, *She is a child. She makes the count. We do not like her counting. We say, "A child did it. It is nothing. Let us count again. Let a man count."*

The women said in their hearts, *Her father is killed. Her mother died. She knows war, what it does.*

Both said, "We saw this sign. Let Siku make the count for us."

Farj said, "This is good. Now we make the count. We play the game of pebbles."

Farj and Siku went to the spring. He was tall, he was proud, he was a leader. She was small, she was a child, a girl child. They put their hands in the water. They took out pebbles, black and yellow and gray. They emptied their gourds. They went to their Kins. They counted deaths, wounds, and blows. For each death they put a black pebble into their gourds. For each wound, a yellow pebble. For each blow, a gray pebble.

They went to the spring. They kneeled down. The Kins stood around them. No one moved. No one breathed. They watched Farj and Siku.

Farj said, "I play black. I play five deaths."

He put his hand in his gourd. He took out five black pebbles. He laid them down in a line.

Siku put her hand in her gourd. She took out black pebbles. She laid them down beside Farj's line. They were five.

Siku said, "I play yellow. I play ten and three more wounds."

She put her hand in her gourd. She took out ten and three more yellow pebbles. She laid them down in a line.

Farj put his hand in his gourd. He took out yellow pebbles. He laid them down beside Siku's line. They were ten and three more.

Farj said, "We play gray. We play blows. We play by one and by one."

Each put their hand in their gourd. By one and by one they laid down gray pebbles. Ten and ten and two more each laid down.

Farj said, "My gourd is empty."

Siku put her hand in her gourd. She took out a gray pebble. She laid it down.

She said, "My gourd is empty."

They rose. They faced each other. Farj was tall, he was proud, he was a leader. Siku was small, a child, a girl child.

Farj said, "Siku, strike me a blow."

Siku struck Farj a blow. With a child's strength she

struck him. He fell down. He howled. He said, "Oh, oh! I am struck with a strong fist! Oh, oh!"

All saw. All heard. None spoke. They said in their hearts, *What is this? What does it mean?*

Farj lay on the ground, a big man, a leader. He howled.

Siku stood over him, a girl, a child. She shook her fist in the air, she triumphed.

A boy laughed. All heard him. They said in their hearts, *This is laughter stuff.* They all laughed. Their laughter was like this:

See, it is the time of rains. The air is thick, it is heavy. Men snarl, they pick fights. Women shrill, they say fierce words to their mates. Children whine, they are bad. Now, see, the rain comes, it goes. The air is light, the earth makes sweet smells. All are happy. All are kind.

Of such sort was the laughter of the two Kins.

Farj rose. He went to the spring. He took out a gray pebble. He laid it down. The lines were equal.

He said, "All is paid. Now we go to Odutu, Odutu below the Mountain. We unswear the War Oath."

10

Mana was foraging by herself. Not far off, Bodu and Nar were standing under a stinkfruit tree, waiting for Tinu to crawl far enough along a branch to knock the fruit down with her fishing stick. Ripe stinkfruit were very soft. If you tried to knock them down by throwing rocks at them they would either burst when you hit them, or when they fell and hit the ground. So the trick was for somebody to climb the tree and knock them down one at a time, while someone else waited below to catch them.

The trick was trickier still this time, because there was a hornets' nest dangling among the ripest fruit, with the hornets coming and going. That was why Tinu was using her fishing stick, so that she didn't get too near. Several of them had kept their fishing sticks because they were useful for a lot of other things besides fishing.

Mana wasn't helping because she didn't much like stinkfruit. Some people thought they were delicious, though even they needed to hold their noses to eat them. She didn't much like hornets either, so she'd gone off to look for something else. Earlier the four of them had been at the end of the line of foragers when Bodu had spotted the tree a little distance away, so Mana was now even farther from the rest of the Kin.

Out on her own like this she went warily, with all

her senses keyed, and paused to peer and sniff and listen each time she moved on. She heard the coming
sounds when they were still far off—someone running,
running desperately, with rasping gasps for air and
unsteady tread. She knew the runner would pass close
by in a moment.

*Stranger comes. Hide. See him. Then choose. Does he
see you?*

That was a rule Mana had been taught from the
moment she'd first known words. She ducked down and
waited. The runner came into sight.

It was a demon woman.

Mana glimpsed only her head and shoulders over
some bushes before the woman vanished behind a larger clump. Beyond the bushes was open ground. Mana
waited for her to reappear. She could still hear the
heavy, exhausted breathing, but no footsteps, so the
woman seemed to have stopped.

At last she burst into sight, a tall, slim, dark woman
whose unbalanced, floundering pace showed how near
she was to the end of her strength. She crossed the open
ground and disappeared again. From the way the
woman was running, her pursuers must be close on her
heels.

Mana stayed where she was. She already knew what
would happen next. How could she help? Run to the
other foragers, beg them to come? There wasn't time.
Besides, most of the men were away, hunting. And anyway they wouldn't come—she'd heard the adults deciding some time ago that what happened between the
marshmen and the demon people was no concern of
the Kin.

All Mana could do was creep in under the bush and
lie there with grief in her heart and wait.

Wait.

The voice of Moonhawk seemed to whisper in her mind.

Almost at once she heard the cries of hunters hot on the trail, staying a little apart from one another so as not to miss the signs if their prey turned aside. They were calling to tell each other as they ran that they had seen some fresh trace. And then their easy breathing and the pad of their footsteps.

Now she saw them, four marshmen, the nearest going past in full view not ten paces from her, the others beyond, moving with the swift lope of huntsmen, smooth and confident, sure that their chase would soon be over. The second man from Mana was the one actually following the trail. Like the woman, he too appeared for a moment over the lower bushes and vanished behind the larger ones, but he came out quickly into the open ground beyond. All four ran out of sight.

Why had the woman stopped with the trackers so close? What had she done there? Rested? No. When a runner rests, gasping for air, the breathing slows, deepens. But hers had quickened, if anything. She had been doing something, doing it in a desperate hurry…

Was she looking for a hiding place? Perhaps, but…

Anyway, Mana had to get back to the others so that they would know where she was. She crawled out and with sickness in her mouth and in her spirit started off for the stinkfruit tree. Nar and Bodu were there, no longer looking up at Tinu but watching the chase. A man's voice shouted in the distance, behind her and to her left. Others joined in, savage and triumphant. The hunt was over. The woman would not have screamed or pleaded for life—she was a demon woman…strange that she had run at all…they'd found her hiding somewhere…a demon woman, lurking and hiding…?

Mana remembered the demon women in the lairs,

facing the Kin when they had come, expecting to be killed and too proud to flinch or show fear.

But this woman had been hiding and had still, as she ran, been looking for somewhere to hide. Not hide herself. Something else. Someone else?

And the whisper in her mind just now hadn't been memory. *Wait*, Moonhawk had said, telling her something as she lay there.

Mana turned and hurried back to where she'd lain, and then moved carefully on, picking the hardest ground, to the farther side of the bushes. Here the soil was sandy, and she could see two sets of tracks—the woman's and the hunter's close beside them. Mana looked to her right. Both sets of tracks vanished at a patch of gravel and then resumed. On the sand, neither set faltered. The woman must have actually stopped on the gravel.

Quickly Mana scanned the area for a way of reaching the place without leaving tracks of her own, but couldn't see one. The hunters would be coming back along the trail soon, looking for what they'd missed, so she ran to the gravel, bent, and lifted aside a low, sweeping branch of the largest bush.

The demon baby was lying there, awake, but not making a sound. He was a boy, about one moon old. He stared at Mana with large, vague eyes as she lifted him out and carried him back the way she'd come.

Nar and Bodu were watching her now from under the stinkfruit tree, but she didn't head for them at once. To confuse the marshmen if she could, she set off toward another patch of bushes, deliberately leaving a few footprints, just as the woman had done. Once there she planned to try to make it look as if she was hiding among the bushes and then go back to the foragers, leaving no trail. As she was nearing the bushes, she heard Nar's warning shout.

"Mana! Marshmen come!"

She turned and ran for the tree. To her left she could see two of the marshmen loping back along the trail. They'd already reached the open area just before the gravel patch. They must have seen her, but the baby was hidden behind her body. In a moment they'd find her footprints and realize she had it. Clutching the baby against her, she raced on.

She was already gasping with the effort when she heard the marshmen's shout. Nar and Bodu were on the far side of the tree now, yelling to the foragers to come and help. She took a quick glance to her left and saw the marshmen racing to cut her off. She was nearer than they were, but they were faster, and closing all the time.

She reached the tree only a few paces ahead of them. She'd run there without thought, because that was where her friends were, but it was only Nar and Bodu, and Tinu up in the tree, against the angry marshmen. Bodu was waving frantically to the foragers. For a moment Mana thought of trying to throw the baby up to Tinu, but it was useless. She knew she hadn't the strength.

She turned and faced the marshmen. It was the only thing to do.

There were two of them. The other two were out of sight. They raised their fishing sticks. Mana could see and smell the fresh blood smearing the vicious points.

"No!" she shouted. "You do not kill him! This is bad, bad!"

They glanced at each other and half lowered their fishing sticks, but Mana could see they were still furiously angry. She didn't recognize them, but she was sure they knew she was Kin, and they wouldn't want to hurt her if they could help it, because the Kin were allies and friends, and if it hadn't been for the Kin the marshpeople would still be hiding in the marshes and living in dread of the demon men.

One of them made the *Give* sound—ordering, not asking—and took a pace toward her, reaching out for the baby as he came. She was backing away when something fell from the tree, right at the man's feet, and burst.

He stopped in his tracks, startled. There was an instant's pause, and a cloud of furious hornets rose roaring around him.

Mana turned and ran. The sudden terror of the hornets gave her a burst of strength. Bodu and Nar were already racing ahead. Someone was running beside her. Tinu. She must have dropped from the tree the moment she'd dislodged the hornets' nest.

But Mana was gasping again. Her knees were starting to buckle. She couldn't see—there was blackness in her head. Her foot caught on something. She stumbled, started to fall, still clutching the baby, trying to twist herself so that she didn't fall on top of him...

A hard arm caught her and held her up. A man's voice grunted. Tor. Then he grunted again on a different note, startled. He'd seen the demon baby.

"What happens?" said several voices together. Mana was unable to speak. Her lungs were dragging the air raspingly in through her throat, her heart was slamming against her rib cage, her head was full of the red darkness. She heard Nar starting to explain what he'd seen—not everything, but enough...

By the time she had recovered a bit and could look around, more than half the foragers had joined the group and the rest were still gathering. Each newcomer needed to be told the story afresh. Mana stood in the middle of them with her head bowed over the baby, not daring to look at their faces. She could tell from the voices that no one was glad of what she'd done. What she heard was doubt, disapproval, anxiety, bewilderment.

There were throbbing patches of pain in her left shoulder and thigh. Hornet stings. She hadn't felt them before.

Now she sensed movements around her, looked, and saw that the four marshmen were approaching and the Kin were grouping to face them. She went and stood behind Bodu, looking over her shoulder but keeping the baby out of sight. All four marshmen were there now. The two in front walked normally, but the third was helping the fourth to hobble along. He was obviously in great pain.

The wound in Tun's arm had gone bad for a while and was still not well, so he'd decided to rest it and not go hunting. Now he gestured to Tor and walked forward with him to greet the marshmen. It looked for a moment as if they were going to shove Tun aside, but he stood his ground with his usual confidence and their leader brusquely returned the greeting.

Then he began to grunt and gesture. His hair bushed out. He shook his stick with a stabbing motion, beckoned with his head to the other three, and once more started to stride past Tun.

Tun moved to bar his way. His hair also bushed, but only partly, showing he was serious but didn't want a fight. The marshman put up a hand to thrust him aside, but Tun caught him by the wrist with his good arm and drew him close, staring down into his eyes, unblinking.

The second marshman hesitated and raised his stick.

The Kin gave a shout and surged forward. Though they were almost all women, these weren't the fawning, servile women the marshmen were used to. They backed off and lowered their sticks. Tun let go of the leader's wrist, and he too took a pace back. His hair settled, and Tun's did the same.

"This is good," Tun said calmly. "We make fire. We eat. We talk. Nar, go find the hunters. They went that way. Say to them, *Come*."

He made the *Come* sound to the marshmen and, without looking to see if they were following, led the way toward a group of shade trees.

While most of the women made fire and prepared a meal, Chogi and Bodu pounded garri leaves and mixed them with a little water to make a paste, which they daubed onto the hornet stings. Though Mana and Tinu had both been stung, they dealt with the marshman first, because he was hurt much the worst. The garri paste didn't cure the pain, but numbed it enough to make it bearable.

By the time Chogi reached Mana, the demon baby was at last beginning to whimper a little and make sucking movements with his lips.

"He is hungry," said Chogi crossly. "Mana, this is stupid. You cannot feed him. You have no milk. He dies."

"Chogi is right," said Zara. "He is a demon baby. One day he is a man. Then he is a demon man. He is not Kin. Let him die now. Give him to the marshmen. This is best."

"The marshmen are friends," said Yova. "Do we make them enemies? This is not good. Give them the baby."

"I say no," said Bodu. "The baby dies—he dies. This is one thing. We give him to the marshmen—we say,

Take him. Kill him. This is another thing. I cannot do this."

"Bodu, this is stupid," said Zara. "This *one thing, other thing*. They are the same. The baby is dead. Do you say to him *Live*, Bodu? You have milk. Do you give it to the demon baby?"

By now Mana was weeping. She looked at Bodu through her tears. The round, cheerful face was frowning. Bodu had been eating well for more than a moon now, and she probably had milk to spare, but nowhere near enough for two babies. And the second one a demon baby?

Mana could see Bodu struggling with Zara's question, and that she couldn't quite bring herself to say yes. It was too much to ask.

There seemed to be only one thing for Mana to do, though it was worse than anything she could have imagined. She stood up.

"I take this from you," she croaked. "It is my stuff. I go away. I go far and far. The baby dies. This is my stuff also."

A voice shouted from behind the women. Po. Mana hadn't realized he'd been listening.

"Mana, I go with you. Your stuff is my stuff. I, Po, say this."

Through a fresh upwelling of tears she heard Tinu's quiet mumble.

"Tinu goes, I go," said Nar. Mana could hear that he had willed himself to say it.

"Suth is hunting," said Bodu slowly. "I know in my heart he says, *We go with Mana*."

"This is stupid, stupid!" cried Zara. "Nar, my son, you do not go! This is not your stuff!"

"Wait," said a voice.

Silence fell. Everyone rose from whatever they'd been doing and turned and stared at Noli. She had been sitting against a tree trunk, feeding Amola, but the baby had let go of the nipple and was waiting like the rest of them, as if she too had recognized the voice of Moonhawk.

After a long pause the voice came again, no more than a whisper but seeming to fill the shadowed space beneath the trees and breathe far out across the sunlit plain beyond.

"His name is Okern."

There was an astonished gasp from every mouth, and then another silence. There was always one person in each Kin to whom their First One came, and that person chose names for newborn babies. So Noli had named Ogad, as well as her own Amola, and long ago she'd also named Tor, after the Moonhawks had rescued him and accepted him into the Kin. She had done this in her own voice, not Moonhawk's.

But it wasn't only that this time she had spoken with Moonhawk's voice. It was the name she'd chosen. The names of babies started with an O sound if they were boys and an A sound if they were girls. Then, when they stopped being babies and became small ones, these sounds were dropped. Mana herself had once been Amana, and Tan had been Otan. When the time came, Ogad would become Gad, and Amola would become Mola. And Okern would become Kern.

Names were repeated. They had to be. There weren't that many possible names to go around. There must have been many Manas before Mana. Some she knew about and some she didn't. But usually there was a gap of several generations between them. Mana had never heard of a name being repeated like this, almost at once, when they could all remember a Kern they had known and loved—a Kern who had been horribly killed, and one of whose killers might have been the father of the baby who now carried his name.

At last Tun rose from where he had been squatting beside the marshmen, treating them as honored guests.

"Moonhawk spoke," he said solemnly. "The boy is Okern. He is Moonhawk. His blood is our blood. This is good. Now I tell the marshmen this. We leave these places. We take the boy. We go far and far. They do not see us again."

He turned back to the marshmen. Mana stood where she was, too bewildered to think, too blinded with tears to see. The baby was struggling now, and on the verge of crying. Somebody touched Mana's arm.

"Mana, give him to me," whispered Bodu. "I have milk. He lives."

Oldtale

The Unswearing

The First Ones spoke to their Kins. They said, "Go now to Odutu, Odutu below the Mountain. Snake and Fat Pig go there. They unswear the War Oath. See this. Let it be done before you all. Then feast."

The Kins hunted. They foraged. The First Ones drove game to the men. They caused trees to bear nuts out of season. They ripened the berries on the bushes and the seed in the grasses. They swelled the rich roots.

The Kins journeyed to Odutu. Their gourds were heavy.

The men of Snake stood before them, and the men of Fat Pig. By two and by two they went to the rock, one from each Kin. They laid their hands upon the rock. They unswore the War Oath.

The Kins rejoiced. They gathered fuel. They built great fires. They roasted flesh, they baked seed paste, they popped nuts. They said, "Come, now we feast. The war is ended."

But the men of Fat Pig said, "It is not enough. Shame is still on us. We have killed a woman. We killed first."

They put Mott in front of them. They took his digging stick from him. They said to the men of Snake, "Kill him."

But the men of Snake said, "Not so. Our shame is greater. Rage was in Mott's heart. He did not see, he did not think, he struck. Ziul chose. He saw Dipu. He said in his heart, *I kill a woman. It is vengeance for Meena.*"

They put Ziul in front of them. They took his digging stick from him. They said to the men of Fat Pig, "Kill him."

Fat Pig and Snake hid in long grasses. They saw this. They went to Black Antelope. They said, "Let there be no more deaths."

Black Antelope put his nostrils to theirs. He breathed out. He gave back their powers.

Fat Pig and Snake made themselves invisible. They went to their Kins. No one saw them. Fat Pig hid Mott. Snake hid Ziul. Their hiding was like this:

See this mountain. A cloud lies upon it. A man climbs. He is in the cloud. It swirls all about him, it is cold, water covers his skin. He cannot see the trail. He is lost.

Such was the hiding of Mott and Ziul. Then Fat Pig and Snake carried them far and far. They were not seen again.

Now the Kins feasted. They were happy.

The First Ones went back to the Mountain, the Mountain above Odutu. They too feasted and were happy.

But Black Antelope said to Snake and Fat Pig, "Let no stoneweed grow in the Places of your two Kins."

They made it so. It is so to this day.

Several moons later, Mana was watching Okern trying to catch Amola. This was difficult for him, as he could only roll, while Amola could already crawl. She was busy with Amola stuff—mostly spotting something that interested her, crawling to get it, and then testing whether it tasted good—so she had no idea what Okern was up to. But he knew.

Now he tried again. He'd almost gotten her the last time, before she'd crawled away to check out a dead leaf. He'd been rolling when she'd moved off, and hadn't seen her go, but she wasn't there when he next looked. Mana saw him frown and gaze around, turning his neat, dark head in little jerks, like the movements of an insect.

Ah, there she was. Patiently he lined himself up for another roll. He hadn't found how to roll in straight lines, so he approached his target in a series of curves, often going in quite the wrong direction before he stopped to check, and then lining himself up again. He was an extremely determined baby.

This is man stuff, thought Mana, smiling. *He has this idea in his head. He will not let it go. This is how men are.*

Then a chill thought struck her. It was a new version of an old thought, one that had lived in the back of her mind ever since the Kin had accepted Okern as one of themselves. Sometimes, as now, it came creeping out to trouble her.

Or is it demon man stuff? Does Okern hunt Amola? One day he would be a man. What kind of a man would he be? A savage killer, like his father? Or strong and gentle like Kern, whose name he bore?

He was a very good baby. Even Chogi said so—at least she said, "For a boy, good. A girl is better." He hardly ever cried, and then quietly, though often he had to wait for food while Bodu and Noli fed their own babies. Mana had to make sure Okern had enough by chewing food for him and spitting it into his mouth. At first he used to spit it straight back, but he got used to it, and she found things he seemed to enjoy and that didn't make his bowels run. She liked to feed him herself, because it was a way of telling him he was hers. From early on he seemed to have decided that she was his, and came gladly to her as soon as one of the other mothers had finished giving him milk.

A prayer formed in her mind. She whispered it under her breath.

> Moonhawk, I praise.
> Moonhawk, I thank.
> See Okern, Moonhawk.
> You gave this name to him.
> Let him be Moonhawk, like Kern.
> Let him not be demon.
> I, Mana, ask.

She sighed and looked around. This was a new camp, right at the far end of the northern slope of the immense valley. From where she sat, Mana could see, rimming the horizon many days' journey to the south, the range of hills they had crossed when they had left the marshes. But they had come here by a far less direct route, for Okern's sake keeping well away from the southern slope, which the returned marshmen were now reclaiming as their own.

Once or twice, as they had slowly explored this new territory, they had glimpsed one of the frightened little black women, but no men. Apart from that, nobody seemed to live here at all.

It was strange. Though not nearly as rich as the southern slope, these were still Good Places. This camp, for instance. It was a fine camp, with two caves and a stream nearby. Why was there no sign of anyone using it?

"The small people had these Places," Chogi had suggested. "They were theirs. The demon men came. They killed the men. They took the women. They are all gone."

It was as good an explanation as anyone could think of.

The camp was as far as they had explored, and it looked as if they wouldn't be able to go much farther. Ahead lay a chain of real mountains, capped with snow. As always, when they first settled at a new camp, Tun had sent scouting parties out to look for possible dangers and good food areas. The mothers, including Mana, had stayed with their babies to forage nearby, gather fuel, and prepare for the evening meal.

The sun was going down, all the other scouts were back, and the meal was ready before Suth and Tor returned. Though they both seemed well, Suth wouldn't talk about where they'd been. He was strangely grave and silent, and Tor kept shaking his head in a troubled way.

When they had finished eating, the leaders of each scouting party stood up and told everyone where they'd been and what they'd found. Suth was the youngest, so he was last.

"I, Suth, speak," he said. "I went with Tor. We went this way...." He pointed directly toward the mountains and went on, describing everything of interest to the Kin—areas of food plants, a place with the right sort of ants' nests, deer tracks, another stream, and so on.

"We found a trail," he said. "It was a people trail. We followed it. We were careful, careful. We saw no one. We came to mountains. The trail went up. We climbed far. There were many trees. They stopped. We came to a valley. It was in the mountains. There we found a thing. I do not tell you now—I do not have words. Tomorrow you see it. Noli comes. It is First One stuff."

That was all he would say, but instead of returning to his place among the men, he beckoned to Noli and took her aside to the edge of the firelight. They settled down and sat talking in low voices for a long while. When Noli came back to the fire she looked puzzled and anxious.

The Kin left early the next morning and traveled east along the route that Suth had described. They weren't exploring, as he and Tor had been, so they made good time and reached the trail he'd told them about well before midday.

It was a well-worn path, broad enough for two people walking side by side, though there were signs that it hadn't been used recently. If they'd turned right they would have been heading for the southern side of the valley, but they went the other way, directly toward the mountains.

Over the past few moons Mana had often seen those white peaks, unreachably far away. Now she was looking at a single one, so close that it seemed to tower above her.

The path began to climb, twisting to and fro. Still

climbing, it entered an area of woodland—not the dense, tangled, steaming forest that grew along the river in the New Good Places, but cool and sweet smelling, with open glades among the trees.

Net and Tor were scouting ahead, with Tun and Suth leading the main group. Mana, Noli, and the rest of Suth's "family" were close behind, with the other members of the Kin spreading down the trail. Sometimes after they'd rounded a bend, Mana could look down and see between the tree trunks the tail-enders still toiling up the previous stretch.

All at once Noli stopped and froze. The others jostled to a halt behind her. Suth and Tun heard the slight commotion and turned to see what was happening.

"Goma is here," said Noli quietly.

They stared at her, then looked at one another, bewildered. Goma was one of the Porcupines, with whom the Kin used to share the New Good Places. She'd been a special friend of Noli's, because Goma was the one to whom their own First One, Porcupine, came. But except for Noli's mate, Tor, who was Porcupine, the Kin had seen nothing of them since they'd split up as they'd journeyed north to escape the drought that was killing the New Good Places. How could Goma be here, after all this time?

"Po," said Noli in the same quiet voice. "Run. Find Tor. Bring him."

Po raced off. Noli waited, gazing up the slope above the trail.

"Goma comes," she said. "Others are with her."

She called the Porcupines' *I come* sound and started to scramble up. Before she'd gone far, someone stole out of the trees above them, peered for a moment, gave a cry of joy and came slithering and bounding down. She flung her arms around Noli and they hugged each other, laughing and crying. Only when they stood apart and gazed at each other could Mana see that this really was Goma.

By then three other women had appeared. Mana recognized two of them as Porcupines. They looked far more scared and uncertain than Goma, until they saw that the people on the trail were their old friends, the Kin, and came down and greeted them.

Then Net, Tor, and Po came hurrying down the trail, and there were still more greetings and cries of gladness, but Mana didn't take much part in them because she was still watching Noli and Goma. She saw Goma admire Amola, and realized at the same moment that Goma's little son wasn't with her. She heard Noli's questioning grunt. Goma's face turned sorrowful and Noli started to weep. He was dead, Mana realized, and wept too.

After that the two women stood for a little while, touching and stroking each other and making murmuring sounds, before they came down and joined the others on the trail.

"What happens to Goma?" Noli said as they climbed on. "I do not know. I feel bad times. I feel sadness. I feel fear, blood, another sadness. My thought is this. The Porcupines come around the marsh. They find little food. Some die. Men come. They fight the Porcupine men. They kill them. They take women, Goma too. They bring her to this place. She is afraid, afraid. It is not the men she fears now. They go. They do not come back. These women are with her. They run away. We find them. Still she is afraid. I feel her fear. I feel the thing she fears. It is demon stuff, bad, bad. Suth says this also."

They climbed on, cautiously now, though they had still seen no sign of anyone using the path for a long while. Then the slope eased, and they came out into a long, narrow clearing. It was the bottom of a valley between two steep ridges of the mountain. Trees clung to the slopes on either side, with dark cliffs above them. A thin stream rippled along the floor of the valley. Some way on, on the left side, the cliff fell sheer down to the clearing. Against it lay a low, treeless mound.

They stopped at the edge of the wood and stood staring. Mana could see no sign of danger, but she could sense something. It was as if the air was full of whispering voices that she couldn't quite hear, while invisible hands were fingering her skin, too softly for her to feel. She shuddered and looked at Okern, but he was fast aleep in the sling Tinu had made for him. His small face was untroubled.

She looked up. Noli was breathing deeply as she sometimes did just before Moonhawk came to her, but there was no froth on her lips and she seemed in full control of her own body. She turned to Yova.

"Yova, take Amola," Noli said. "This is my stuff. It is Goma's stuff. We go first."

Goma was already beside her, looking anxious and frightened, but she took Noli's hand and together they led the way on. The Kin followed, keeping close together, but the three women who had been with Goma in the wood refused to come any farther.

The trail ran straight toward the mound, which lay on the far side of a low rise, so that they saw only the upper half of it until they reached the top of the rise. By then they were only a few tens of paces from it, so that its meaning burst suddenly upon them.

Just in front of them, two large boulders stood on either side of the trail, forming an entrance. On top of each of them was a human skull. Rings of skulls circled their bases. Beyond the boulders, two lines of posts topped with skulls led down to the mound. More posts and skulls ringed the mound. Where the path reached the mound there was a low slab of rock. Behind it, in the mound itself, was a dark opening.

Noli paused, but not from uncertainty. She seemed to be waiting for something. She looked at Goma, who was holding herself more confidently now. They nodded, as if one of them had spoken.

"Moonhawk is here," said Noli, still quietly. "Porcupine also. He slept. Now he wakes."

The two women, still holding hands, walked on toward the mound. The Kin followed, spreading out into a line on either side of the path, but Suth and Tun stayed on it, and Mana followed them down.

When Noli and Goma were about ten and ten paces from the slab, a man came out of the opening behind it. He was old. His hair was white, his eyes bloodshot and gummy, and he used a staff to walk with, though he held himself as straight as a young man. Mana didn't need the color of his skin or the skulls that dangled from his belt to tell her that this was a demon man. She would have known by the way he moved, by the look on his face, by the feel of his presence. Though he was old and feeble, he seemed far more terrible than any of the savage young hunters they had fought in the marshes.

The red-rimmed eyes stared at the newcomers. The man raised his staff and gave a harsh, croaking cry, which echoed from the cliff above him.

He waited for the echo to die, and cried again, and then again. Each time the cliff repeated the sound. Mana's stomach felt cold inside her. The echoes sounded to her like more than echoes. They sounded like the demon speaking from the rock.

The Kin murmured uneasily. She guessed they were having the same thought, the same dread. Then Okern stirred against her side. She looked down and saw that he had awakened and was gazing around with a puzzled frown.

Had the demon spoken to him too? Especially to him? Called to him?

No!

Now Mana knew what she must do, why she was here. She moved forward, and Po started to come with her.

"Wait," she whispered. "This is my stuff. It is good."

She walked steadily forward, past Tun and Suth, past Noli and Goma, and up to the slab. The mad old eyes stared furiously at her, then fell on Okern.

The man's face changed completely. His mouth opened in a horrible grin, showing a few yellow teeth. He made a puffing sound and started to hobble around the slab.

Mana waited, standing her ground, until he stood facing her.

"No, you do not have him," she said firmly.

"Do not have him," whispered the cliff.

The old man poked his head forward at her and made an angry gesture toward the slab—*Put the boy there*.

"No," said Mana again, and the cliff answered, "No."

The man took a tottering pace toward her, reaching out an arm to grab at Okern. Mana snatched him away. She was filled with sudden fury, fury at this fearsome old man, and all the demon men, and what they were—what they had allowed themselves to become. It had been their choice. The demon was theirs. They had chosen it.

"No!" she yelled. "He is not yours! He is mine! He is Moonhawk!"

"Moonhawk," shouted the cliff.

The old man staggered. It was as if the echo itself had struck him a violent blow. He clutched at his staff with both hands, fighting for balance. His mouth gaped. A grating retch rasped through his throat. He staggered again, as if another blow had struck him, and toppled forward at Mana's feet.

She stayed where she was, staring down at him, clutching Okern to her side, until Tun came forward, bent, and rolled the old man onto his back.

"He is dead," he announced.

"Dead," agreed the cliff, matter-of-factly.

Moving and speaking quietly so as not to wake the echo, they carried the body into the hole in the mound. They dragged out some strange stuff they found in there—old fighting sticks, horns of antelope, twisted bits of tree root, and bundles of dried grass tied into curious shapes. Almost everything had at least one skull lashed to it.

They laid the skulls aside and piled everything else in the entrance to the hole. Again setting the skulls aside, they pulled up the ring of poles and the posts beside the path and added them to the pile. Then they set fire to it.

At first Mana took no part in any of this but sat cradling Okern in her arms, touching, stroking, murmuring softly to him, as she had so often seen the Porcupine mothers doing with their babies. Slowly she realized that something had changed inside her.

Her wound was healed, the wound in her spirit that she had given herself when she had killed the demon man in the marsh. Clean spirit had grown over the place, leaving no scar. It was finding Okern that had healed her—saving him from the marshmen, mothering him and caring for him and watching him begin to grow into a life of his own, and now, finally, bringing him here and facing the old demon man, and the demon itself, and defeating them.

She had killed a man. He had been bad, bad, but he had been people.

But she had saved a man, and not just his life. If the Kin had never fought the demon men, or if the demon men had won that war, Okern would still have been born, but nameless. And he would have grown to manhood learning to be a demon man like his father, so that was what he would have become, a hunter of people, a savage killer of men. Now, perhaps, he would grow up not like that.

Mana had long had a secret fear that Okern's real father had been the very man she had killed. Now, though she would never know, she found herself hoping it might be so.

This, she thought, was what Moonhawk must have meant when she'd told her to wait.

After a while Noli came to feed Okern, so Mana passed him over and went to help the others carry the skulls and pile them up away from the mound. They were just finishing when Noli came to give Okern back. As soon as Mana took him he fitted himself snugly against her, sighed, and fell asleep.

"Noli," she said, "I thank. And I say this. My trouble is gone. I am well."

"This is good," said Noli. "Now we do the death dance for all these people. Mana, you dance with the women."

So Mana joined the line on one side of the pile of skulls, and stamped out the dance, and sang the long wavering wail that would free any spirits that were left in this demon-haunted valley and allow them to go wherever they were meant to by whatever First Ones had been theirs. Even at this distance their voices roused the echo in the cliff, so that it seemed to be taking part in the ritual.

By the time they'd finished, it was almost nightfall. They had brought enough to eat at midday, but they had neither foraged nor hunted, and there was little left. They wouldn't take any food from this demon-infected place, let alone sleep here, so they made their way back down through the wood in the dark to a stream a little below it. There they drank and laired for the night.

Mana slept with Okern close beside her, sheltering him with her body, warming him with her warmth, and did not dream at all.

Several more moons later the Kin was once again at Two Caves. Most of the Good Places on these northern hills now had names of their own. Not long ago Mana had heard Po telling Tan a wonderful story about why Snakeskin Hill was called that. It wasn't the real reason, it was just something Po had dreamed up. Po was always full of dreams.

By now Amola could stand and was starting to walk, while Okern was crawling so fast and with such determination that Mana needed to keep an eye on him all the time he wasn't asleep. He seemed to have no sense of fear or danger.

Noli and Mana were alone at the camp. Noli had stayed to soak and pound a blueroot she'd found so that it would be ready for the Big Moon feast the next night—a serious feast, because tomorrow would be Nar's last day as a child. The morning after, he would have the first man scars cut in his cheeks and become a man, and he and Tinu could then be mates.

Mana was there to keep Noli company, something

she especially needed just now because Tor had been away so long. He and Goma had gone to make their way south and see if they could find any more of the Porcupines lingering around the edges of the marsh. This was their second expedition. The first time they'd found a man and a woman, mates, and their two children, who'd somehow managed to survive.

Noli was sure there must be more. Mana didn't really understand why she said so—it was First One stuff. When Mana had confronted the old demon man at the Place That Was Not Spoken Of, Noli said Porcupine had been there. The demon men had brought Goma and the other women to the valley to look after the old man, but the demon in the cliff had been too strong for Porcupine, because all his people were scattered in different places. But Porcupine was still around, and with Moonhawk to help him he had come back. He couldn't have done that, Noli said, if everyone except Goma and the other two women had been dead.

So now Mana was helping with the blueroot, and Amola was also helping after her fashion, pounding a bit of rind with a rock Noli had given her. Okern had to have a rock too, of course, but he didn't care what he pounded, as long as he could do it good and hard.

Noli paused in her work to regather the blueroot on the flat rock she was using to pound on. Amola heard the break in the steady rhythm of pounding and looked up. Her lips moved. Mana could see she was trying to ask something. Noli laughed delightedly.

"Mana, Amola has words!" she cried. "She says, *Ma?* She asks, *Mother, why do you stop?* Oh, she has words, Mana, she has words!"

This was a question the Kin had discussed endlessly from the moment Amola had been born, but more since she'd stopped being a wrinkled little blob of a baby and had gotten a face of her own. Then it became easy to see that she was like Tor in some ways, with his fine bones and high cheeks, but had Noli's mouth and chin, while her skin color was in between theirs. So would Amola be like Noli and have words, or be like Tor and have none, or be somewhere in between, with just a few?

Noli, after that single syllable, was certain of the answer.

Mana laughed with her, happy in her delight. Then her eye fell on Okern, who had taken his rock to the cave and was hammering away at the cliff beside it. He would hammer the whole hill away if he could, she thought. Yes, and he could do that before he could speak to me. He will never say *Ma* to me. She bowed her head, biting her lip.

"Mana, you are sad," said Noli. "Why is this?"

"Okern does not have words," said Mana.

"He is clever. He is strong. He is brave. He is beautiful," said Noli.

"Noli, this is true," said Mana. She was in fact very proud of Okern's good looks. But she shook her head again.

"Hear me, Noli," she said hesitantly, thinking it through as she spoke. "Say in your heart, *Okern has words*. Now say this. *One day Okern is a small one. Then his name changes. He is Kern. But he understands little. He gets big, he is a boy. Now he understands more. Now I, Mana, say to him, 'Kern, I am not your true mother. She is dead. She did such and such things. Your father is dead. He did such and such things.'*

"Noli, I do not say, *Your mother was a demon woman. Your father was a demon man.*

"Then I, Mana, say, '*I found you. Moonhawk took you in. Now, Kern, choose. Which are you? Are you like your father and mother? Are you like me, Moonhawk? Think, Kern. Then choose.'*

"Noli, I can never say this to him. He can never choose. He does not have words."

Noli put down her rock, and came and squatted beside her and took her hand.

"Mana," she said. "Okern is people. One day he chooses. Now, see Goma. She is good, good. She says in her heart, *This is good. I do it. This is bad. I do not do it.* She does not need words for this. She is people.

"Mana, *good* is a word. *Bad* is a word. But they are more, more. They are...I do not know what they are, but they are people stuff."

Mana looked at Okern. *Yes, he is people*, she thought. And Noli is right. She remembered the sudden rage that had surged through her at the Place That Was Not Spoken Of, at the thought that the demon men had chosen to be what they were. *That rage came from Moonhawk*, she thought. It was what had allowed her to stand up to the old demon man, and shout defiance to his face.

Yes, good or bad—whether he learned the truth about his own parents or not—Okern would one day choose.

That was people stuff.